On Wings Of Love

by

Cynthia Harrod-Eagles

Dales Large Print Books
Long Preston, North Yorkshire,
England.

British Library Cataloguing in Publication Data.

Harrod-Eagles, Cynthia
  On wings of love.

A catalogue record for this book is
available from the British Library

  ISBN 1-85389-443-5 pbk

First published in Great Britain by Sphere Books Ltd., 1978

Published in Large Print December, 1995 by arrangement
with Severn House Publishers Ltd.

Dales Large Print is an imprint of
Library Magna Books Ltd.
Printed and bound in Great Britain by
T.J. Press (Padstow) Ltd., Cornwall, PL28 8RW.

CHAPTER 1

Suffolk is a green county, the greenest county in England. It is green even in winter, when trees shrug off their responsibility to the general colour-scheme. But greenness means wetness, and wetness means rain. On the whole, the people of Wesslingham didn't mind the rain—even liked it. As Mrs Partridge at the Bell said, it's God's rain after all. But too much, even of a good thing, can be depressing, and it had been raining now for three months almost non-stop. People were beginning to grumble.

Kestrel Richards was not one of them. Since she had come home from her job in Lowestoft for the last time, after being made redundant, she had been indestructibly happy, and she was often to be seen striding down the main village street, bare-headed in the rain, whistling like a blackbird.

Kestrel lived with her widowed father in a small cottage on the edge of Wessle Marsh.

5

The cottage was called Coats Cottage, but Mr Richards, who was a Suffolk man born and bred, said that the name was nothing to do with wearing apparel, but was the way local people pronounced 'coots', of which there were a large number on the marsh. It certainly explained why the signpost at their turning off the main street said in wobbly and faded letters 'To Marsh and Coots Cottage'.

Birds of all sorts were Mr Richards' life. He was an ornithologist of some repute, and though he had officially retired, he still wrote articles for East Anglian papers and parish magazines and did an occasional broadcast for the radio's nature programme 'Out and About'. He had written many books, including his most famous work on endangered species, *The Precious Few*, which had won the Conservation Society's award one year.

Though he loved all birds, his speciality was the hawk and falcon families, which was why, of course, Kestrel had been given that name. She was his only child, and he adored her. He had brought her up almost single-handed, for her mother had died when she was only four, so it was perhaps inevitable that she should absorb

6

his love for birds. He had been astonished when on leaving school she had insisted on taking a secretarial course, and having passed that with flying colours had got herself an office job.

'Why on earth,' he had asked her in his mild way, 'should you want to shut yourself up in an office all day when you've the whole of Suffolk to wander in?'

'It isn't that I want to, Dad,' she had said firmly, 'but I must earn my living.'

'I can't see why,' he said, waving a vague hand round the house. 'We've everything we want here. The house—the garden—our own vegetables—and my royalties are enough to support us for the things we can't grow or catch.'

'It can't support us for ever,' she had said. 'Besides, Dad, I'm a girl. I want some of the things other girls have, like pretty clothes and shoes, and we can't afford those things on your royalties.'

'Well, since you say so I have to believe you, but I really can't see what you want with pretty clothes—you've nowhere to wear them.'

'That's precisely it,' Kestrel had said grimly. 'I'm happy enough in gumboots and jeans, but just now and then I'd like to look pretty.'

'You always look very beautiful to me,' said Mr Richards, and it was no more than the truth.

But Kestrel had been adamant, and had got herself a job, and had worked hard, and had even at times enjoyed it. She liked the company of other girls, and she liked being able to look round the shops in her lunch hour, but she knew it wasn't really for her. She *did* dislike being shut up all day, and she found the other girls' ignorance of wild life and nature in general as odd as they found her ignorance of pop stars and television programmes.

So she had not even pretended to be sorry when she was made redundant. As soon as she had got home after her last day she had torn off her work clothes, scrambled into her comfortable old jeans and jersey and gumboots, and gone out for a long tramp through the marshes and woods.

Her father had been delighted that she was home. 'Don't be in any hurry to get another job,' he had said. 'We don't need money that urgently. Spring's coming on, and there'll be plenty to eat from the

8

garden, and you know the vicar's very kind in the matter of eggs from his hens.'

'I won't be in any hurry,' Kestrel promised him. 'I suppose I'll have to get another job, but not for a month or two. I've my redundancy money to keep me going, and I can do odd jobs around the village. I'm just so glad to be home.'

'Good, good, then you can come with me on my little journeyings. There's so much to see at this time of year—and if you feel the need to keep in practice with your typing,' he added innocently, 'you can always type up my notes for me. I find my fingers getting slower all the time.'

'Of course I'll do your notes for you, Dad,' Kestrel laughed. 'Don't I always?'

One of the first things she had to do was to replenish the larder, for when she was working and unable to shop except at weekends her father tended to empty the food stores that she had painfully built up, without thinking of buying fresh. So she set out the next morning with her purse and basket to walk the half mile into the village proper.

The first part of the journey lay along the narrow, high-hedged lane that led nowhere but to their cottage. At the corner of that lane and the village street was the small red-brick house called, from time out of mind, Dodman's, so that the corner was called Dodman's Corner. It was inhabited by one old man in his nineties, whom Kestrel had always thought of as Mr Dodman, though his name was really Ambrose. Dodman was local dialect for snail, and the old man moved very slowly.

He was in his garden as she came past, and called out cheerfully to her.

'Mornin', Miss Kestrel,' he said, coming down the path to the gate. His broad vowels made the name sound like 'Castrol', but she was well used to that. Few of the local people said her name right. Mostly they pronounced it 'Kesterl', and as a child all her playmates had called her 'Kester'.

'Hello, Mr Ambrose. Lovely day, isn't it?' She saw his hand go instinctively to his pocket and then fall away again reluctantly. Every school morning through her childhood she had walked past Dodman's, and he had come down to the gate with something in his pocket for her, an apple or plum or biscuit. The habit died hard, even though nowadays he had nothing he could give her.

'Lovely day all right, thank the Lord,' he said piously, before adding, 'only we could do with a bit of dry weather. How are you down by the marsh? Bit wet, eh? Not come in over the doorstep yet, eh?'

'Not yet,' she smiled. 'The ducks are liking it.'

'Ar,' he nodded. 'Birds never mind a drop er rain. So you're back now, eh? Goin' ter help yer dad fer a bit, 'stead of runnin' off to town all the time?'

'Just for a while,' she agreed easily. 'I must say it's nice not to have to travel in every day. It's like a holiday for me. Though I shall have to get a job eventually.'

Ambrose shook his head. 'Never knew the like,' he said sadly, 'young girls workin' all hours. Wasn't done in my day.'

Kestrel forbore to point out that in his day most young girls had gone into service and worked far longer and harder than she ever had. It was never worth while disputing points like that. He finished his think and then smiled sunnily and toothlessly at her.

'Summer visitors'll be comin' down soon. Be plenty of work hereabouts fer

11

y' then. No need to go traipsin' off to town again.'

'You could be right,' she agreed with him cheerfully. She knew that he was only concerned that she should stay put, and wanted to reassure him. After a moment or two she walked on down the road towards the village, but the thought of the summer visitors was in her mind. Wesslingham didn't have much to attract tourists, and beyond the occasional visitor passing through and stopping the night at the Bell they saw few strangers. A few miles from the village, however, was a group of holiday chalets, which families hired out for a week or two in the summer. These holidaymakers brought much-needed extra trade to the village shops and pubs, and a welcome new topic of conversation.

Kestrel liked the advent of new faces in that brief season, for there was no doubt that, lovely though Wesslingham was, it was rather short of young people, particularly young unmarried people...

Having done her shopping and chatted to all the people who wanted to say how glad they were to see 'Miss Castrol' back (it makes me sound like a garage beauty queen, she thought) Kestrel finished off her village tour by dropping into the craft shop for a cup of coffee.

The café part of the craft shop was not open until summer, when the visitors came, but Kestrel was very friendly with the lady who owned the shop, and there was always a cup of something on the go. The lady's name was Theodora Bielecki, but she was known universally and at her own request as Theo. She painted a little, turned pots, carved things out of wood, made soft toys, embroidered, and made costume jewellery out of copper and enamel. All these things she sold in her shop.

Apart from this she was an expert on Wesslingham Ancient and Modern, was a pillar of the church, and lived a satisfying mysterious double life that involved trips up to Norwich and even, it was whispered with bated breath in the post office, to *London*. Kestrel didn't know what it was that Theo did for a living—apart from the shop which evidently didn't entirely support her—but she never asked, feeling that if Theo wanted her to know she would tell her.

Theo was glad to see her, and greeted her with the words,

13

'Jolly good! The coffee's just perking. Take a pew. I was just embroidering a hassock.' She made a large gesture towards a lovely thing of plum-coloured velvet with delicate gold threads across it which she had put down as Kestrel came in. 'The Vicar was showing me some of the old Victorian ones in the vestry—put aside when the moth got at them—so I thought I'd try my hand at it.'

'It's lovely, Theo, really. He'll be delighted.'

'Oh—I hadn't thought of giving it to him—didn't think it would be good enough—do you really think he'd like it?' Theo blinked, a little confused.

'Of course he would. Those leather ones are beastly, and so hard.'

'Supposed to be hard, I should think—penance, mortifying the flesh and so on,' Theo said. 'Well, I heard you were back. Jolly good thing too. You were never meant to stooge away in a stuffy old office for a living.'

Kestrel laughed. 'Isn't it funny how everyone seems to think I was destined for higher things? One has to earn a living, you know, however one dislikes it.'

'Life's too short to spend it doing things

you don't like,' Theo said firmly. 'Look at me, for instance.' Kestrel waited with bated breath, but Theo changed tack. 'Anyway, what are you going to do next?'

'Nothing for the moment, just help Dad and take a breather while I look round. I've got my redundancy pay to spend before I need worry about money.'

'Hmm. Difficult. Pity you can't write like your Dad. Still, you'll be getting married some day, and then you won't need to worry about a job—your husband will keep you.'

'How do you know he will?' Kestrel asked, amused.

'Well, why on earth get married otherwise?' Theo said innocently, and Kestrel really couldn't tell if she was joking or not. However, she replied,

'Oh, I don't suppose I'll ever get married. After all, I never meet anyone marriageable. Who is there in Wesslingham? The only unmarried man is old Mr Ambrose, and he's ninety-three.'

'I see your problem,' Theo said with a twinkling eye. 'Never mind, there's always the summer visitors to look forward to.'

'Poor summer visitors, they don't know what they're in for,' she smiled.

'What do you mean?' asked Theo.

'Ever since I came home,' Kestrel said, 'people have been promising me the summer visitors for one thing or another. I can't imagine how we manage for the rest of the year.'

She finished her coffee and stood up. 'Off home?' Theo asked.

'Not yet. I've got to see a woman about a rabbit,' Kestrel said mysteriously.

'Oh—Laura at the library. Well, give her my regards,' Theo nodded. 'Drop in again next time you're passing.'

'I will,' Kestrel smiled, and went out into the rain which had just begun again.

Wesslingham Library was a very imposing building for so small a village, for in fact it served four other hamlets and the mobile library as well. It was housed in a beautiful red-and-white brick Georgian house just past the Bell. It had been neglected for many years after the war, until its shelves had been lined with little else but ancient volumes of Ruby M Ayres and Clarence E Mulford. And then Laura came along.

Laura Holmes was a 'foreigner'—that is, she was not Suffolk-born, nor even an East Anglian—and she brought to her position as librarian of Wesslingham a totally foreign

16

drive and energy. She engaged in vigorous battles with the local authorities, got her budget increased to almost double, threw out almost all the stock, and began to rebuild. As a result, nearly ten years later, the library had become a centre of village community life as important in its way as the church or the post office.

Kestrel remembered the gloomy, dingy place of her childhood as she went into the entrance hall, bright with spring flowers in floor-boxes and with fresh paint, and into the library proper with its fine selection of clean, up-to-date books on well-lit shelves. Laura herself was just arranging her week's special selection on the trolley by the door. She ruled Wesslingham's literary taste with a gentle but despotic hand, and what she recommended usually got read.

'Hello, Laura—how are you? Kestrel greeted her. There was no-one in the library at that moment, so she didn't bother to whisper.

'Oh, keeping busy,' Laura replied, straightening just enough to look at Kestrel over her shoulder. 'Though sometimes I wonder if it's at all worth it. Mrs Dorrit just brought me back *Jane Eyre* and told me it wasn't as good as the television version.'

Kestrel laughed. 'Look at it this way,' she said. 'Ten years ago no-one in the village would have known there *was* a book version.'

'I suppose you could be right. Anyway, what can I do for you? Something to read on the bus?—or did you pop in to see how many times your Dad's book's been out this week?'

'Neither, actually—I wondered if you could let me have a rabbit for our tea.'

Laura lived in a tiny bungalow on another spur of the marsh, about half a mile from Coats Cottage as the crow flies. Though her bungalow was small her garden, stretching right out into the rushes, was enormous, and Laura supplemented her income by growing vast quantities of vegetables and by keeping rabbits for sale. Kestrel was always a little shy of asking for a rabbit, for Laura seemed to be very attached to them, and Kestrel suspected she cried a little when one went for the stew pot.

'I'm afraid I haven't one at the moment— not one of my own, that is,' Laura said now, and Kestrel thought her dark eyes gleamed a little with relief behind her tinted glasses, 'but I've a wild rabbit you could have, if you're interested. It would stew all right, I should think.'

'What did it die of?' Kestrel asked warily, and Laura grinned suddenly.

'Mortal wounds,' she said. 'Larch brought it in. I don't know if he killed it at a stroke, or killed it bringing it to me to make better, but it was dead on arrival, as they say in hospitals.' Larch was Laura's Siamese cat, an enormous, burly animal and a ferocious hunter.

'Well, yes, I'll have it, if Larch won't object.'

'Oh, he wouldn't eat it. I had to teach him not to kill my rabbits, of course, and he still isn't sure of the distinction with wild ones. He was very anxious about the wild one when he brought it in—kept apologising for breaking it.'

'Poor Larch,' Kestrel said. 'Can't you put bells on yours, or something, so's he can tell the difference?'

'That's an idea—I hadn't thought of that,' Laura said thoughtfully. 'Though mind you, there probably won't be many wild rabbits around for him to be puzzled by—not now that hawk's arrived.'

'Hawk?' Kestrel said, immediately alert. 'What hawk?'

19

'Oh, I've seen it a couple of times, flying low over the reeds—hunting, early in the morning when I've been out for mushrooms. I saw it yesterday in fact—had something that looked like a baby rabbit in its claws, though it could have been a rat, I suppose.'

'That's interesting—I must find out if Dad has seen it,' Kestrel said. 'Whereabouts did you see it?'

'Yesterday? Oh, it was over the reed beds, more or less between your place and mine. A kind of reddy-coloured hawk.'

Kestrel shook her head. 'I don't know what that could be. I'll ask Dad—he's bound to know. Well, thanks, Laura—and what about the rabbit?'

'You can fetch it on your way home if you like. It's hanging up in my shed. You know where the key is, don't you?'

'Everybody knows where the key is,' Kestrel laughed. 'I really don't know why you don't leave it unlocked.'

'Old habit,' Laura said stiffly. 'You never know who might be passing by.'

'And how much do you want for it?' Kestrel asked, feeling for her purse.

'Oh, I don't want anything for it. Larch didn't charge me. You might save your bacon rinds for him, if you want to say thank you to him.'

'I'll do that,' Kestrel said. 'I'll drop them in to you.'

'Preferably in a paper bag,' Laura said, straight-faced.

'Spoilsport. Cheerio, then!'

'Cheerio. And tell your Dad, if he wants to sell his bird books, he'll have to work a shark into the story somehow,' Laura called after Kestrel, adding as she reached the door, 'or a plane crash. That's what sells.'

Kestrel waved in reply, laughing, and went on her way.

CHAPTER 2

The rabbit was so small and thin that Kestrel decided it would have to be helped to make up a stew, so instead of cutting across the marshes the short way home she went back into the village to buy a half pound of bacon, and went home via the roads.

As she reached Dodman's Corner she

21

saw the vicar's motorbike up against the wall of Dodman's, and as she came up to it the vicar himself came out of the house, accompanied by old Mr Ambrose.

'Ah, there she is,' Mr Ambrose exclaimed, catching sight of Kestrel. 'Speak of the devil—sorry, Vicar.'

'Hello, Mr Truman,' Kestrel greeted him.

'Hello, Kestrel, my dear—I was just on my way up to Coats Cottage.'

'To see me, or Dad?'

'Both, my dear, of course. Perhaps I could offer you a pillion ride?'

Kestrel eyed the bike dubiously. 'If I were you, I should wheel it down. Our road isn't much, after all this rain.'

'Yes, of course, being so low-lying,' the vicar agreed. 'I wonder whether we'll be getting any drier weather soon.'

'The forecast on the radio said more rain,' Kestrel said. Mr Ambrose, who had been looking from one to the other, made his exit with the contemptuous comment,

'Huh, we don't never get anything good off them forecasts. We useter get better weather when we got it orf the birds and spiders and suchlike.'

The vicar watched the old man shuffling

22

back up the garden path and then turned to Kestrel with a rather worried expression. 'Do you really think,' he asked in a low voice, 'that he believes the weather is *caused* by the forecasts? Because if he does I really ought to—a point of such fundamental importance—'

'I think he was pulling your leg,' Kestrel said firmly. 'Shall we go? Dad will have the kettle on by now, and we can have a cup of tea.'

'Yes, of course, you must be getting wet. Thoughtless of me. I hear you've given up your job in town—tell me, what are you thinking of doing now?' He retrieved his bike and Kestrel fell in beside him as they walked up the narrow lane, talking amicably.

Coats Cottage was a welcoming sight on a grey, rainy day, with smoke coming out of its tall chimney, conjuring up thoughts of tea and hot toast, but despite this the vicar stopped short of the cottage and stared out over the marsh with an expression of great pleasure.

'What a lovely view you have of the church from here,' he said. Kestrel stopped beside him and looked out over the olive-grey expanse of reed and water towards

23

the square church tower. 'You know, every time I come down here I always wish that I could paint. So stark and compelling—' He might have fallen into a brown study, oblivious of the rain running down inside his collar, had not Mr Richards opened the door to the house at that moment and called them.

'Are you coming in, Vicar? The kettle's on.'

In the hallway Kestrel dragged off her gumboots and anorak and added them to the general heap of muddy outdoor clothing that always silted up the hall. She wondered for a moment what it would be like to live all the time in the town, where you could go out even in bad weather and never get muddy. Then she shook the thought out of her head and the rain out of her hair, and followed the vicar into her father's study, where a fire was always kept going to keep the damp from the books.

Kestrel loved this room best of all the rooms in the house. Two walls were lined with books from floor to ceiling, and the other two, painted white, were decorated with some of her father's best bird sketches, lovingly sandwiched between

24

two thin sheets of glass and bound with passe-partout by Kestrel herself, when a child. There was a big fire of logs and coal in the high, arched red-brick fireplace, and its cheerful light fell on old but well-polished furniture. The single window looked out over the marsh, and the padded window seat in front of it had been Kestrel's favourite seat as a little girl. When, after her mother died, she had felt lonely and had sought him out, he had set her in the window seat with one of his bird books that had coloured illustrations, and she had stayed quiet there while he worked at his desk. It must have been then, she thought, that she first began to love birds.

'Now then, Mr Truman, sit down, sit down. I'll make some tea,' her father was saying.

'No, it's all right, Dad, I'll do it. I have to unpack my basket anyway,' Kestrel said. 'I'm sure you two have a lot to talk about.' The vicar was a keen amateur bird-watcher, and often came up to consult her father. And that reminded her of Laura's 'hawk'. 'Oh, and I have something to tell you—but I'll get the tea first.'

25

'I have something to tell you, too,' Mr Truman said, 'but I'll wait until you come back with the tea, Kestrel—I'm sure it will interest you too.'

Kestrel nodded and took herself off to the kitchen, wondering if perhaps the vicar's news was the same as hers. When she eventually came back with the tea tray, however, he was talking about the altar-cloth that Theo had embroidered.

'It really is most beautiful. Such lovely flowers, and so delicately worked. Of course, we can't use it until after Lent, as I've explained to her, but we shall certainly have it out then. Have you seen it, Kestrel?'

'Yes, I was there when she gave it to you, after choir-practice last week.'

'Of course you were—silly of me.'

Kestrel sat down and began to pour out. Glancing up from her task, she said,

'What was the piece of news you have for us, Mr Truman?'

'Ah yes, my news. Well now, you know, this *may* be rather exciting. It was something I saw yesterday, when I was on my way up to the church for early mass. Of course, it isn't often we get anyone in for early mass when the mornings are as

26

dark as this, but I say it all the same. I think it was a much better system in the old days, when the times for mass were set by the sunrise, so that—'

'Yes, of course, but what was it you saw?' Mr Richards interrupted, for the vicar was rather prone to get carried away, so to speak, by his church.

'I beg your pardon—what did I see? Well, just at first, you know, I thought it was a dog, a brown dog, running very fast through the reeds, you know the way a dog runs when it's got its nose down to something. And then it came nearer, and I saw that it was in fact a bird.'

He looked round at them, gathering their attention like a true narrator.

'It was skimming low over the reeds, beating back and forth very fast, and it made now and then a beautiful, shrill cry—I can't imitate it.'

'What did it look like?' Mr Richards asked. He was alert, almost tense.

'It was like a small hawk, a reddish brown in colour, and the noticeable thing was that it had a grey tail and grey flashes on its wings.'

Kestrel heard her father let out his breath in a long hiss. She turned to him.

27

'My news was more or less the same, Dad. Laura at the library told me she'd seen a strange bird yesterday morning, hunting over the reeds. She said it was like a reddy-coloured hawk. I said I'd ask you what it could be.'

'I looked it up straight away in my bird book when I got home,' the vicar went on, with a trace of excitement in his voice, 'and the only thing I could find that was at all like it was—a marsh harrier.'

'A marsh harrier,' Mr Richards said in a low, almost reverent voice.

'I've never heard of it,' Kestrel said. Her father looked at her sharply.

'I would be surprised if you had, really. It's a very rare bird, very rare indeed. In fact it's only seen nowadays in Minsmere. It used to be a very common bird in Anglia, but it's very sensitive to noise or disturbance around its nesting sites, and there are few places now remote enough from civilisation to attract it. Not only that, but its numbers have been severely reduced by chemical pesticides and sprays.' He looked from Kestrel to Mr Truman and back. 'It would be very very exciting—very exciting *indeed*—if one were to be found

28

hunting on our marsh.'

'Do you think it is possible?' Mr Truman asked. Mr Richards got up from his seat and fetched a book from his bookcase before answering. Kestrel knew the book by its size and colour—it was his own work. *The Precious Few.*

'Of course it is possible,' he said. He sat down and turned the pages carefully, and then passed it, open, to the vicar. 'Kestrel, get me Brown off the top shelf,' he said. Kestrel got down the familiar big book and handed it to her father, who again turned the pages and then gave it back open, this time to her.

'The thing that makes me hopeful,' he said, 'is that the harrier is very distinctive—there's no other bird that is commonly mistaken for it. The grey tail and wing patches are quite unmistakable.'

Kestrel meanwhile was looking at the picture her father had given her, a full-page colour plate of a beautiful brown hawk with a grey hood and breast, its yellow eyes glaring fiercely back from the page at her. She read the caption and saw that this was the female.

'It's lovely,' she said, and looked up at her father. 'Oh I *do* hope it is a marsh harrier. It would be really wonderful for you.'

'I think perhaps it would be Mr Truman's discovery,' Mr Richards said politely.

'Oh, by no means, sir, by no means. If it is what we hope it is, I want no credit. Without your presence here in the village I would never have been more than a putter-out of crumbs for robins. Besides, it will be for you positively to identify it, and that, I am sure, will take much lying around in damp grass. My sighting was purely fortuitous.'

'And Laura's,' Kestrel added. 'I suppose, if it is what you think it is, it will be because Wessle Marsh is so little overlooked. After all, apart from us and the church, there's only Laura's bungalow that actually overlooks the marsh. And a good thing too, if the harrier is as sensitive to noise as you say.'

'I don't think,' her father said, almost severely, 'you ought to put any hope at all on its breeding here. Such a thing hasn't been known for—I can't remember exactly how long, but fifteen years or so. They don't breed in this country except for a very few secluded places.

No, this will just be an odd bird that has stopped off here to hunt for a few days.'

'In that case,' the vicar said, 'you had better try to see it as soon as possible. It might be off at any time. It might,' the possibility occurred to him, and his voice sank in disappointment, 'have gone already.'

'Laura said she's seen it a couple of times, so it must have been here a few days,' Kestrel remembered. 'She said she saw it yesterday with a baby rabbit—or it might have been a rat.'

'I don't think it would be a rabbit—too large a prey I should have thought,' the vicar said doubtfully, looking at Mr Richards for confirmation.

'Well, she does wear tinted glasses,' Kestrel said vaguely. Her father shot her a piercing look, and then laughed aloud.

'Kestrel, my dear, how unscientific you can be,' he said. She smiled back at him, seeing how pleased and excited he really was. After all, not only was he an ornithologist, but a specialist in hawks and falcons. If this really was a marsh harrier, it would be about the best thing that could happen to him.

31

'Shall we go out tonight and look for it?' she asked.

'At sunset, of course,' he replied.

'I only wish I could come with you, but I have an evening service to do over in Southwick,' said Mr Truman. 'However, I'm sure you'll let me know the result of your watch, won't you?'

He sounded hesitant, as if, thought Kestrel, they would keep the secret to themselves and refuse to tell him anything!

'Of course we will,' she said. 'I'll be at morning service tomorrow anyway, and I'll tell you then if we've seen anything.'

'Is tomorrow Sunday?' Mr Richards said with vague surprise. 'Well, I may come myself, then, if there's anything to tell.'

The vicar blinked in surprise at that, and then smiled happily.

'Then I must hope doubly hard for good news,' he said with a twinkling eye. 'It must be two years at least since I had the pleasure of seeing you at church.'

'Well,' said Mr Richards, taking this in his stride, 'after your generosity in coming to me with this news, it's the least I can do.'

And the two men smiled, understanding each other perfectly.

CHAPTER 3

Late in the afternoon it stopped raining, and it looked as though there would be a fine sunset.

'I'm glad of that,' Kestrel said to her father as they put their jackets on. 'Not that I mind the rain, but if the clouds are thick it gets dark before sunset, and then there's nothing to see.'

'There's never *nothing* to see,' Mr Richards said reprovingly. 'One creature's bad weather is another creature's good.'

Kestrel smiled patiently. Her father was sometimes *too* literal. 'Anyway,' she said, 'if I get my hair wet much more often, it will grow even faster, and I'll have to get it shorn instead of cut.'

They went out into the golden light of the afternoon, stepping oozily through the mud of their yard, and Kestrel thought that this was not everyone's ideal way to spend a Saturday night. But then the excitement of the possibility of a marsh harrier pushed every other thought out of her head.

And of course her father was right—there was such a lot to see. This was the time of day when the rabbits came out to feed, when the small night hunters began to wake up and move about, when birds of all sorts held their daily congregations. Starlings and rooks had their own particular trees which they filled with noise. No-one was certain what purpose these meetings served—Kestrel had her own idea, but it was 'unscientific' so she never told her father.

She glanced at him as he walked ahead of her, noticing anew how softly he walked, how much in his element he was. His keen, alert eyes were the only parts of him that moved quickly—the rest of his body seemed to glide through the tall grasses without disturbing them. She had no idea of the picture she presented, of course, but when her father glanced back at her once on their journey, he thought how much like a wild animal she looked, perhaps like some kind of big cat in the undergrowth.

When they reached the reed beds near Laura's bungalow, they stopped, Mr Richards indicating that this was a likely place from which to watch. They settled down in the driest places they could find. Mr Richards got out his binoculars and set them down beside him ready, and then they both froze.

After a while the wild grew used to them being there, and things began to flow back around them. Kestrel saw a tiny vole run past in jerks, pausing only a few inches from her to stare and twitch before running on. A blue heron waded with his stilted stride through the water a little ahead of them, and paused, one foot up, to swipe at an itch on his chest with his long, sword-like bill. The sun was going down, and its deep light gilded a halo round the bird. Kestrel wondered what it would be like to be in the marshes of the Camargue at this time of day, and see that same gilded-halo effect on a flock of rosy flamingoes.

And then she became aware that she was not alone. Moving her head very slightly she glanced down, and saw a pair of vivid blue eyes glaring at her from the reeds. She almost started, but controlled herself in time as she realised that it was only Laura's cat Larch. Damn, she thought, he'll ruin everything. If he's hunting, he'll put up all the birds in the area. We might as well move on—we'll see nothing here.

Larch's body oozed after his eyes, very

slowly, until he was standing beside her, crouched low, nothing moving except the very tip of his tail which flicked, twice. Kestrel made a threatening face at him, and his mouth opened very wide in a miaou, but he made no sound. Kestrel's eyes went back to the heron to see if it had been disturbed, and when she looked back again Larch had gone, as silently as he came.

Kestrel glanced across at her father, wondering whether to tell him that they had a rival in the area, but at that moment his eyes swung urgently towards her and then away, and she realised that his whole body was pointing like a setter in one direction. And then she, too, saw it.

A bird, winging low over the reed beds, about a hundred yards away. It swept the length of one bed and then whirled up at the end of its flight and as it tilted its wing to turn, Kestrel saw the bright flash of grey on the brown feathers. It mounted the air, turning back the way it had come with its unmistakable hawk-like flight, and then dropped to beat back across the reeds again.

Kestrel looked again at her father, hoping he might confirm to her that it was the

36

harrier, but his eyes were fixed on the bird with such intensity that she knew he had forgotten she was there. She watched again.

Now the flight pattern had changed. The bird climbed the air, spiralling slightly to gain height, until he was perhaps two hundred feet up, and then he seemed to fall, like a dead thing. Kestrel's heart was in her mouth—she had not heard a shot, but one could shoot from downwind without being heard. But her anxiety lasted only a fraction of a second, for the bird somersaulted in its fall, caught the wind again, and beat up to repeat the trick.

For the next few minutes it entranced its hidden watchers with a dazzling display of aerial acrobatics, plunging, whirling, twisting, somersaulting, and sending, after each display, its shrill 'kwee-a' echoing over the marsh. It was a sight and a sound that Kestrel could never forget, and she was held breathless, unaware of anything, until with a last, haunting cry the bird flew away out of sight.

Then she gradually came back to earth, realising that she was very cold and stiff with remaining in the same position for so long, and that her feet and her backside were wet from crouching in the damp. Still from old discipline, she waited until she saw her father move before she cautiously straightened up, stretching each of her limbs in turn and groaning softly.

Mr Richards turned a glowing face to her. His eyes shone with a light of absolute joy, and she didn't need to ask if the bird was, indeed, a harrier.

'It was beautiful, Dad,' she said instead. 'Absolutely beautiful.'

'Do you know what we've just witnessed?' he asked her. She waited to be told. 'Those acrobatics were the marsh harrier's mating ritual.' He looked over his shoulder as if expecting the bird still to be there. 'There must be a pair of them.'

'Really?'

Mr Richards looked slightly amused. 'My dear, the harrier would hardly perform the mating ritual on his own.'

Kestrel smiled wickedly. 'Perhaps it was a rehearsal.' Her father ignored that.

'The question is, will they mate here? It would be—quite wonderful if they were to mate and nest here—but I suppose it's too much to hope for. However, I shall certainly keep a close eye on them.'

'We'd better get back and dry out,'

Kestrel said, taking his arm affectionately, 'and get some supper. I can see that you'll be spending most of your time in the wet grass from now on, so I'd better make sure I feed you while I can.'

They turned and began to walk back again, and when they had gone only a few steps, Larch appeared again, falling in beside them and keeping pace with them like a dog. He had what appeared to be a shrew in his mouth—dead, Kestrel was glad to notice.

'Hello, Larch,' she said. He didn't look up, but growled threateningly at her, though the resonance of the warning was somewhat muffled by the mouthful of fur he held.

'Did you see him earlier on, Dad?' Kestrel asked. 'He came past me just when the harrier first appeared. I was afraid he'd scare everything away, but he was very quiet.'

Her father smiled at her. 'He came past me, too,' he said. 'He was sitting a few feet away from me all the time, as still as a statue. I have an idea he was bird-watching himself. A very rare character—I salute him.'

Their way home led close to Laura's

bungalow, and as they approached it, still accompanied by the cat, they saw Laura herself at the bottom of her garden, digging over another patch to plant with vegetables. Larch veered off to join her, calling her loudly and obscurely through the shrew, and Laura looked up and waved.

'I've just seen that bird again,' she called as soon as they were near enough to hear her. She stooped automatically to take the offering from the cat, examine it briefly, and give it back.

'So have we,' Kestrel replied. 'We've been watching it doing a Red Baron stunt—absolutely unbelievable. Your cat was there too—Dad says he was bird-watching himself.'

'I was saying what a rare thing it was to find a cat who likes bird-watching,' Mr Richards said solemnly. Laura laughed, leaning on her shovel.

'He knows when he's beaten,' she said. 'He once tried to get fresh with a swan, and he's never forgotten it. He has a healthy respect for any bird larger than a sparrow now.'

'I'm glad to hear it,' said Mr Richards.

'Dad thinks the bird might be going to

mate,' Kestrel explained. 'And it's a very rare bird indeed, so it would be awful if it mated and then got eaten by Larch.'

'I'll have a talk with him,' Laura promised. 'I'm very glad for you, anyway, that it turned out to be something good. What's it called, for interest's sake?'

'A marsh harrier,' Kestrel told her. She nodded.

'I'll look it up on Monday morning. Might do a frieze on it for the children's library.'

'Oh no,' Kestrel said, alarmed, 'please don't do that. In fact, if you wouldn't mind, we'd prefer you didn't tell anyone about it—it's a very shy bird and it might be scared off.'

'Well, all right, if you think so, I won't mention it. Pity not to share the excitement, but I suppose you know best.' Laura took her weight off her shovel, and began to dig again. 'You'd better catch your father up—he looks as if he wants his tea.'

Oh dear, thought Kestrel, I've offended her. She hesitated for a moment, and then with an inward shrug she waved her hand and went after her father. She'll get over it, I dare say. I'll pop in and see her on Monday morning, and have a chat with her.

Kestrel intended getting up early on Sunday morning to go and have another look at the bird, but she overslept and was only up in time to get ready for morning service. Although it was not far across the marshes to the church, it was quite a long walk by the road, and she had to go by road so as not to get muddy, for she was in the choir, and therefore on display. She did, however, take jeans and a pair of plimsolls with her in a carrier bag so that, having done her duty, she could at least come back via the marsh and have a chance of seeing the rare visitor again.

It was raining again, a thin, fine rain that seemed, if possible, wetter than the other sort. Kestrel, however, was too happy to mind it, and sang as she walked up the road towards Dodman's Corner. She sang her favourite hymns, which were inappropriate to the time of year—but she always felt that Lenten hymns were dull. She chose instead the military kind of hymns, like 'For All The Saints' and 'To Be a Pilgrim', which had a good swinging rhythm to walk to.

She walked down the village street, past the Post Office, past the Bell and Theo's shop, past the library and the Dog and Duck, singing, but thinking all the time of the strange bird. Had she known she was being watched at some point on that walk she might not have sung so loudly and unrestrainedly, but she didn't know it.

After the service she stopped to tell the vicar the good news, and he shook her hand and congratulated her so vigorously that Mrs Dorrit almost fell over trying to hear what it was she was being congratulated about, her mind running inevitably on weddings.

'I suppose your father will be writing an article on it for the parish magazine?' Mr Truman said. 'And possibly a piece for the radio as well?'

'I suppose he will eventually,' Kestrel replied. 'But I think for the moment he's happy enough just watching it. I expect he'll be out there somewhere now.' She remembered what had been said yesterday and added, 'It looks as though you'll have to wait another two years before you see him in church again.'

Mr Truman sighed good-naturedly. 'At least I know that he does carry on with

43

his devotions, even if he doesn't come to church for the purpose. Well, well, you'll let me know if anything further develops?'

'Of course,' Kestrel said. 'I'm just going to change into my jeans now and then I'll walk back home that way.'

'Have you your boots with you? No? I do hope you won't catch harm from getting wet.'

'It wouldn't be the first time I'd got wet this year,' Kestrel laughed. 'If it doesn't stop raining soon we'll all have to think about arks.'

Reaching the edge of the marsh, the part behind the church that was fenced off from the road by a post-and-rails, Kestrel rolled up her jeans to the knee and climbed between the bars of the fence. At once she put her foot down a hole, and as well as the inevitable water and a lot of mud, a stone rolled into her plimsoll and wedged under the instep. She almost cursed, remembered it was Sunday, and sat down by the fence on the driest bit of ground she could see to take off her shoe.

Having shaken out the stone, she was about to put the shoe on again when a bird

44

flew down to land on one of the posts and she glanced up to see, only feet from her, a harrier.

She froze, but her heart was beating fast. The bird turned its head alertly, eyes staring, golden eyes in a pale face, and Kestrel realised all at once that this was a female—proof, if proof were needed, that there was a pair of them! The bird had in its beak a clump of dried vegetation—grass and weed tangled together with mud—the kind of natural rubbish with which marsh birds make their nests.

The bird flew off, and Kestrel, frantic with haste, dragged on her plimsoll blindly while she kept her eye on the harrier, trying to see where it went. She got to her feet and began, as unobtrusively as possible, to follow.

It was a long, slow business tracking the bird, for she had to be careful not to frighten it. It flew backwards and forwards, collecting dried grasses and taking them back to the nest site, and each time stopping somewhere en route, as it had stopped on the fence post, to look around for danger. How it had not seen Kestrel that time she didn't know, but she offered up a prayer of thanks.

Eventually, about an hour later, she had tracked the bird to a large reed bed beside an outcrop of waste land, and, crouching behind an oil drum, she at last saw the bird adding the latest sample to a growing pile of reed straw which was to be its nest.

'Wait till I tell Dad about this,' she thought to herself. 'The harrier actually nesting! This will make history!'

She watched for a long time, and was rewarded in the end for her patience by a sight of both birds, for the male came to the nest site with a small water-snake hanging from its beak, a sign that its hunting had been successful. It must have reminded the female that she was hungry, for a moment later she flew off with the male, and there was soon the sound of their shrill 'kwee-a' hunting cry.

Kestrel too was hungry—she glanced at her watch and saw that it was past lunchtime—and she straightened up and started out across the waste land as a convenient way home. She passed out through the makeshift gateway under a large hoarding which she had never bothered to read. She wondered suddenly what was this piece of land next to which the harriers had chosen to nest, and glancing up at it she saw, with horror, the name of the largest building firm in that region.

'Another major development by Cossey's' said the board.

CHAPTER 4

'I dunno, my duck,' said Joe Lambert, landlord of the Dog and Duck, looking at Kestrel over the top of the glass he was wiping. He was only five feet tall, and since he was also rather stout he gave the impression of being absolutely circular. 'You shoulder gone down the Bell if you wanted to know about Cossey's—their son Bill works for them—don't he, Phil?'

'Eh?' Phil the barman looked up from the pint he was drawing.

'Bill Partridge works for Cossey's.'

'Over to Southwick, last I heard. Why'n't yer ask him?' Joe turned back to Kestrel with a merry eye.

'I'd never recommend anyone to go down the Bell, not if they was nearer here. What'll you have? On me—since I

47

don't see you in here very often.'

'Don't make me feel guilty, Joe,' Kestrel said. 'You know I always get up too early to be out late at nights.'

'Well, tonight's the exception, then, i'n'it? What'll it be?'

'Oh, I'll have a half with you, thanks very much,' Kestrel said. She had come into the village with the sole intention of finding out what she could about the building site—what was planned for it, and when. It seemed a stroke of unnecessary irony that the harriers had chosen to build in that very spot. She had hurried home at lunchtime to tell her father everything, and having spent an afternoon watching, he had confirmed her findings—the birds *were* nesting, but any activity on the building site would put an end to that, and they would not nest again that year.

Before she had got her job in Lowestoft, Kestrel had been quite a regular visitor to the Dog and Duck. In the summer they had live music there at weekends, a folk-singer with a guitar, or piano and drums, whatever could be had, and Kestrel had sometimes even helped behind the bar. So it seemed to be the obvious place to go to gather information, and here she was.

As Joe put the half-pint before her, her attention was attracted by someone on the other side of the bar.

'Hey, Kester, fancy a game of darts, then?'

She looked across, and saw Tim O'Connor, standing poised with a dart in his hand, obviously having come in too early for any of his usual companions. She picked up her glass and walked across.

'Hello, Tim. All right, I'll play, but I haven't had a game for a long time, so I'll be a bit rusty.'

'Don't worry, I won't laugh,' Tim said, apparently forgetting that when she had been a regular player here a few years back she had beaten him every time he dared to play with her. Tim O'Connor had been at school with Kestrel back in the village school days. He had lived in Wesslingham all his life, as she had, and his aunt, Miss O'Connor, was very active in the Women's Institute. Kestrel had never liked him much, from the time when he was about ten and she had caught him stealing birds' eggs. He had a firm scorn for all forms of bird life, and for that reason alone they would never be very good friends.

49

They started their game, and as Kestrel took her first shot Tim leaned against a table and made conversation.

'Well, I see you're not married yet, then,' he said, having apparently racked his brains and found nothing else suitable to say. 'When'll we be hearing the wedding bells for you? Eh?'

It was the kind of question that she had to parry politely from all the village elders, since they believed any female over eighteen ought to be married, but she didn't see why she need have it from Tim as well.

'That's not a very sensible thing for you to ask, is it, Tim? Considering you're the only other one in our class at school who's managed to avoid the noose.'

Tim looked slightly uncomfortable. 'Noose? That's not a nice way to talk about marriage, is it?'

'Well, what would you call it? I've heard you saying much the same kind of thing yourself in the past.'

'Ah, but it's different for a feller,' he said, stepping forward to take his own shot. Kestrel smiled pityingly.

'Poor old Tim—so old-fashioned! So far behind the times.' Tim muffed his last

50

throw, and the dart hit the wire with a clang and bounced back to his feet.

'What do you mean?' he said defensively, picking up the dart and handing it to Kestrel.

'Haven't you ever heard of equality for women?' she asked pleasantly, throwing the darts. Tim snorted.

'You won't find much of that round these parts. Anyway,' he hastily changed the subject, 'what're you asking about Cossey's for? What's the interest all of a sudden?' He thought of something, and his face beamed. 'Thinking of getting a job with them—brick-laying?'

'I might just do that,' she replied evenly. 'I could fancy being a hoddy.' She knew he would jump onto this and begin an argument about the physical differences between men and women, and she wanted to keep him away from her interest in the building site. He was the kind of person who might well go along there, if he knew about the harriers, and throw stones at them. Not for spite, but just to see if it was true that they would be frightened.

She finished her game with Tim, and excusing herself on the grounds that she had to be up early the next day, she left the Dog and Duck and went along to the Bell, hoping to see Bill Partridge.

'No, love, he's out tonight. Got a young lady out by Kessingland, he has,' said Mrs Partridge pleasantly. 'Been going steady nearly two months now,' she added with pride, and Kestrel saw the inevitable question in the lady's eye but was unable to forestall it.

'When are you going to bring us home a nice young man, then? We all quite thought you must have someone out in Lowestoft. I remember Mrs Dorrit saying a while back that only a town boy would be good enough for you—though anyone might say the same, seeing as there's no boys in Wesslingham at all not married, unless you count Tim O'Connor, and he's such a tearaway I wouldn't wish my worst enemy's daughter to marry him—oh, excuse me a minute, love.'

Luckily at that moment a customer attracted her eye down the bar, and when she came back her general flow had been diverted.

'Now, what was it you wanted to ask Bill about? P'raps I can take a message?'

'Well, not really,' Kestrel said. 'I just thought, with him working for Cossey's, he might know something about that cleared site down at the end of the village—past Three Trees and before the railway line.'

'Lord love you, of course he does. He'll be working there himself tomorrow. Ten Georgian-style residences, that's what that's to be. They've had the work on the books for ever so long, but there's been so much rain about they've never been able to start it. There was a gentleman here—oh, there's another customer—excuse me, my dear.'

When she came back again she had evidently forgotten again what it was she was saying, and said merely,

'Why don't you pop down there tomorrow and have a word with Bill. He'll tell you what you want to know, I'm sure.'

'Yes, I will. Thanks, Mrs Partridge,' Kestrel said, and turned away to make her way home, a little worried. Still, if the rain had held everything up so far, it might well continue to do so. No sense in worrying about it tonight, not till you know what's what, she told herself, but it didn't stop her worrying all the same.

On Monday morning she went to the building site via the village, for her father

53

had letters for her to post. Early though she was, the post office was already busy, and she had to wait her turn behind several people, one of whom, she saw with sinking heart, was Mrs Dorrit, the village's Olympic-standard talker. The other people waiting didn't mind being behind Mrs Dorrit, for they were in no hurry, and besides, Mrs D's one virtue was that when she gossiped she did it loud enough for everyone to hear.

'Ever such a nice young man, Mrs Partridge says—real nice dresser, and talks nicely—you know the kind of thing. Ever such lovely manners, too—well, they do, don't they? Come from Norwich—' she looked about her and nodded to emphasise the importance of that bit.

'Well, how long's he staying?' asked Mrs Baldergammon, the postmaster's wife.

'He ha'n't said. He was staying over at the Crown in Southwick, so he must be well off—'

'Not if he's here on business,' Mr Baldergammon interrupted. 'If he was on business, his company would pay, so he could stay where he liked.'

Mrs Dorrit was not to be cheated of his wealth. 'Well, if he's working for a company 'at can afford to let him stay at the Crown, then he must be getting good wages, so he must be well off.' Mr Baldergammon allowed her that one, mainly because he was involved with paying out Mr Ambrose's pension.

'Anyway,' Mrs Dorrit went on, seeing she was going to get no more opposition, 'he moved over to the Bell, it being more convenient for him, you see, and there he is now. Ever so nice—good-looking and all—and no trouble at all, so Mrs Partridge says—like one of the family, she says. Only,' her voice took on an indescribable sadness, 'only I suppose he's married, being as old as he is and well-off with it.'

She glanced round at Kestrel as she said that, and Kestrel looked firmly into the middle distance and refused to be drawn in. Objectionable man, she thought, coming here with his nice manners and his nice accent, so that Mrs Dorrit can bait me all the more. Any stranger that came into the village was automatically held up against Kestrel for size, and she was getting a little tired of it. How long, she wondered, before I'm left alone like Theo and Laura? But then, their cases were not exactly parallel, since neither of them were Wesslingham born.

Seeing that the next person in the queue before Mr Baldergammon's position was Mr Barrow, Kestrel joined the other queue. Mr Barrow and the postmaster were both marrow-growers, and their arguments over the rival merits of their monster plants could stretch out over an hour or more. Kestrel bought her stamps from Mrs Baldergammon with such firmness that the postmistress had only time to wonder wistfully why the stranger had come to Wesslingham at this time of year and be assured that Kestrel did not know (and by the tone of her voice cared less). Then at last she was out and walking briskly down the village street in the Southwick direction.

When she arrived at the waste ground, she found that already things had been happening. A load of bricks had been delivered and dumped just inside the yard, and Bill Partridge, alone on the site, was laboriously stacking them at one side. Kestrel's eyes jumped to the marshes, and to her unspeakable relief she saw a quick brown flash as one of the harriers took flight. So they were still there!

'Hullo, Kesterl,' Bill said amiably, stopping work as he saw her and walking across. 'Heard you was back—not working that is. Cigarette?'

Kestrel shook her head and waited while he lit one for himself before saying,

'Bill, what is all this?' she waved a hand round the cleared site. 'What's going on here?'

'Cossey's,' he said succinctly, 'Ten town houses. Bought the site last September, they say, but what with the weather and one thing and another—well, they haven't been able to do anything. Still, with spring coming on, things'll start moving.'

Quickly, urgently, Kestrel told him about the birds.

'I did notice one of 'em when I got here this morning,' he said amiably. 'Never took no notice one way or the other really—a bird's a bird, and 'tis only a bird after all.'

Kestrel explained, passionately, that this was more than just a bird. 'Any noise or disturbance and they'll leave, they won't nest here. The disturbance will put them off nesting at all this year, and they'll never come back. It may be the only chance we'll ever have of getting this bird back to its

57

natural habitat. Oh, can't you see how important it is?'

Bill Partridge looked at her impassioned face, screwing up his brown eyes against the smoke of his cigarette. 'I can see that it's important to you, all right,' he said sympathetically, 'and I don't mind keeping away from them. You see I'm only stacking bricks this morning, and I can stay over this side of the yard and not go near 'em—but it won't do no good. The cement mixer'll be here later this week, and then there'll be noise enough.'

'This week?' she said, aghast.

'Don't you know the agent's here?' Bill said. 'Come from Norwich, just to see this site gets under way. He'll hurry things along all right. He was stopping over the Crown, but when I told him about Mum's cooking and all, he changed and come over ours. He's in the big front room over the garage—what I painted just after Christmas, and Mum put the new curtains in what she got the material at the jumble sale in St Patricks.' He had his mother's love of circumstantial detail.

So that was what the stranger was doing here, Kestrel thought bitterly. Well, he must be made to see his error—nothing,

58

nothing was going to stop the harriers nesting, if she had to throw herself into the cement mixer to stop it. Wild plans flitted through her head, and she turned her face away towards the marsh, looking for the harriers as she thought.

It began to rain again.

'Looks like He's on your side, anyway,' Bill said, glancing upwards. He stubbed out his cigarette and turned away. 'Well, I'll just stack a few more, and then I'll be off. Looks as though it's going to come on heavy, so there won't be much done today.'

'You'll remember—about keeping over this side, won't you, Bill?' Kestrel said, coming out of her reverie.

'Don't worry about me, Kesterl—I wun't hurt your birds. But I'm only one. Can't say for the rest.'

'Thanks anyway, Bill,' Kestrel said, and, sticking her hands in her pockets, walked gloomily away.

She stopped on her way back to make her peace with Laura, but found that she had already forgotten her momentary annoyance of the day before, and invited Kestrel back to the bungalow for lunch. Kestrel agreed happily, and didn't much mind when she found it was a working lunch, which meant bread and cheese and tea in the garden while they finished the digging Laura had started the day before.

'How are your birds,' Laura remembered to ask. Kestrel told her. 'That's bad. Dear me. Well, I must hope for your sake the rain continues to fall, though if it does we'll get a rotten potato harvest, not to mention the onions.'

'There seems to be no pleasing farmers,' Kestrel said, digging savagely, to relieve her feelings about the building site. 'Last year with the drought they were saying it would be a poor potato harvest, and now they'll say it was the rain.'

'Sensitive things, potatoes. Don't like to be disturbed at nesting time,' Laura said, and Kestrel glared at her so that she took a step backwards and lifted her hands, 'Hey, don't go for my throat. I was only being funny.'

'Sorry,' Kestrel said, a little shame-faced. 'But this is too important to joke about.'

'Kestrel, my child, nothing's too important to joke about. That's how fanatics are born. And by the way,' Laura added, straight-faced, 'if ever you fall in love, make sure you get angry with the bloke now and then—you look very impressive.'

And at that Kestrel had to laugh, and dug on less violently and with more pleasure.

When Laura's lunch break ended, Kestrel walked back with her to the library, and spent a while there looking at some books until, seeing that the rain had eased off, she decided to go back via the marshes and the reed bed to see if the harriers were still there.

She approached the nesting site via the building site, and as she reached the gateway, she saw that, though Bill had evidently gone home, someone was in the yard.

It was a tall man's figure, a man wearing the kind of smart raincoat that only a town-dweller would possess, and wellington boots that were either new or had been *cleaned* since they were last worn, for there was no mud on them. So she didn't need to see the theodolite in his hand to know that it was her arch-enemy, the agent from Norwich.

Kestrel's blood boiled at the mere sight of him, and with her lips pressed firmly together and her nostrils flaring, she marched into the builders' yard to do battle.

CHAPTER 5

Stuart King had never been keen on the Wesslingham job. Not that there was any question of him refusing it—he was good at his job and earned good money, but he was not so much his own master that he could say yes or no to any particular assignment. But he knew that the job would be troublesome, and he had not relished the idea.

Stuart was a man who admired order, neatness, efficiency. He was born and brought up in a town—Norwich, as it happened—and he admired the efficiency with which a town operated, each person doing his little bit towards the smooth running of the whole. The country struck him as being untidy and inefficient in the extreme. Large tracts of land stood unused and unusable. People worked peculiar hours and could never be found when they were wanted. Tools and machinery were left lying around until they rusted or got lost.

Certainly some of the products were useful and enjoyable. Cows converted grass to milk, but in such a slow and wasteful way, grazing erratically over huge fields and leaving manure in places where it couldn't be collected and used. No, the country was a mystery to him, and he preferred that it should stay that way.

Then there was the Wesslingham job itself—that was going to cause trouble. There is a kind of natural rhythm to a building job, and once you lose it, everything goes wrong. This job was already six months behind schedule, and that was a bad sign. Mind you, there were some compensations to being here—he had found a very nice, motherly sort of landlady in Mrs Partridge at the Bell, his room was comfortable, and his meals, which he took with the family in the back kitchen were delicious and plentiful. He was a rather shy, diffident person in his private life (one of the reasons he was still, at twenty-seven, unmarried) and he was glad to have found a place to stay where the people were kind to him.

But of all the trouble he had expected, he had never imagined that on his first day on site he would be attacked by the Wild Woman of Borneo. That was his first thought as Kestrel marched up to him, and he might be forgiven for taking one step backwards before he controlled himself and put on his politest face.

His second thought was that this muddy, wet and dishevelled Wild Woman was extremely beautiful in a ferocious sort of way, with her blazing blue eyes and her curling chestnut hair tangled by the wind and dewed with raindrops. However, admiration didn't seem to be one of the things she wanted, and as she stopped in front of him, glaring at him, he could only ask, rather feebly,

'Were you looking for someone?'

To Kestrel the voice sounded faint and bored, the sort of world weary voice of a person too sophisticated to be bothered with the natives.

'Are you the agent?' she asked belligerently.

'Er—yes. I have that honour,' he said cautiously.

'Well, you can't build here.'

'Why not?' was his natural reaction, before he even wondered who she was to tell him so.

'You simply can't, that's all. It's pre-posterous.'

'Oh,' Stuart said, beginning to see the light. She wasn't someone in authority, she was some kind of protest organiser. The country seemed to be rife with them—mostly women without enough to do—all eager to prevent people from carrying on with their jobs for silly reasons. 'And would you like to tell me why?' he asked, humouring her.

'Over there,' Kestrel said passionately, pointing a quivering finger towards the marshes, 'over there, just on the edge of this piece of land, a pair of marsh harriers have started to build their nest.'

'Oh, birds,' he interrupted, enlightened. The tone of his voice breathed super-ciliousness to Kestrel, who immediately bristled.

'Yes, birds. Of course, *you* wouldn't know anything about birds, but this part of Suffolk is a natural breeding ground for a lot of rare species. It's one of the few parts of England that haven't been overrun with industrialists and speculators building housing estates to line their own pockets. And for that reason we do get rare birds here, some of them birds which won't nest

65

anywhere in England now.'

'And I suppose your—whatever it was—is one of those,' Stuart said, still politely, despite her disparagement of what she thought he was.

'My "whatever it was" is a pair of marsh harriers, a very rare and very beautiful bird of the hawk family. They used to be common in these parts, but they've been poisoned with chemicals and driven away by industry, and now they are only visitors here. They only breed in one or two protected colonies. None of them have bred here on Wessle Marsh for fifteen years.'

'Well now they *have* nested, I should have thought you'd be happy.'

'That's the whole point,' Kestrel said, exasperated. 'I've told you they've been driven away by industry. They're very sensitive to any kind of noise or disturbance while they're nesting. Any attempt by you to build on this site would drive them away. They wouldn't nest at all this year, and would never come back again.'

'Pardon me—but you are—?' Stuart asked at this point, to gain time.

'I'm Kestrel Richards, and my father is Graham Richards, the ornithologist.' He

66

had obviously never heard of the name.

'Oh,' he said. 'I thought perhaps you were some kind of official of a preservation society, or something like that.'

'Well, I'm not, but I don't see what difference that makes.'

'Oh none—none—of course.' When he was nervous, his voice sounded more than ever bored, and Kestrel had no chance to cool down. 'And you live in Wesslingham?'

'Over there,' she said abruptly, pointing. 'Coats Cottage, on the edge of the marsh. Now what are you going to do about it?'

'About what?'

'About the building site, of course. You see why you can't build here.'

Stuart began to get a little angry at her tone of voice. 'I don't propose to do anything other than what I am here to do—which is to see that this building project goes ahead with all possible speed. I sympathise with your feelings for your bird—'

'It isn't just me,' Kestrel almost shouted at his stupidity. 'It's the concern of everyone in the village. It's a matter of concern for the whole country. To do anything to put a breeding pair of marsh harriers in jeopardy would be a crime against posterity.'

'Fine words,' Stuart said irritably, 'but I've never heard of this bird and I doubt whether anyone else outside of a small handful of bird cranks has—'

'Bird cranks!' Kestrel was almost speechless with rage.

'—and I don't see my bosses being moved by the consideration of a bird which, since nobody has ever heard of it, nobody will ever miss.'

The two of them stared at each other, Kestrel red-faced with rage, Stuart tall, firm and icy with determination. It was an obvious impasse, and after a moment or two Kestrel turned on her heel and marched away through the rain, leaving Stuart, though she didn't know it, rather shaken.

'My dear, you are in a state,' Mr Richards said mildly as Kestrel came in, banging the door after her. He happened to be crossing the hall at the time, and took in her dishevelled appearance without concern, since he was used to her being wet and covered with mud. But he couldn't ignore the red patches on her cheeks and the line of white fury round her nostrils. 'What has happened? Come into my study—you're wetter even than usual, I think.'

'Ooh, that pompous pig, that ignorant, conceited butcher, that—'

'Kestrel, do calm down!' Mr Richards said. 'You quite alarm me.'

'I can't help it, Dad—I'm so mad I could spit.'

'You look it,' Mr Richards said, laughing at her. 'Whoever it was annoyed you ought to be shaking in his shoes. You look like a savage of some kind—very dangerous.'

'Do I?' Kestrel paused, thinking of the neat, almost elegant appearance of the opposition. She looked down at herself, took in the muddy jeans, the huge gumboots weighted down with clay, the torn anorak—not quite the height of feminine elegance. She looked in the small and spotty mirror on the wall beside the coat hooks, and noted the tangle of wet hair with bits of dried grass sticking out of it, the un-made-up face with a streak of mud down one cheek—however had that got there?—and a new kind of redness suffused her cheeks.

Whatever must he have thought of me? she wondered. I look about fourteen, like one of those horse-mad girls that hangs around stables. Most certainly *not* an impressive sight. No wonder he didn't take me seriously. I look an absolute sight!

Subdued now, she took off her boots and anorak and followed her father into the study and went to stand in front of the fire to dry out the back of her jeans—always the wettest part of her owing to her habit of sitting in the grass in all weathers to watch birds.

'I ought to get a pair of those plastic pants they put on babies,' she said. Her father smiled, glad that she had got back her sense of humour.

'Just let me put the kettle on, and you can tell me what all the fuss and feathers was about,' Mr Richards said, and on his return Kestrel told him, calmly, about her meeting with the agent.

'And the net result is that the building will start as soon as the rain lets up. Oh, Dad, we must *do* something!'

'Well, Kestrel, I don't see really what we can do. The man has a perfect right to build where he chooses, so long as he has planning permission.'

'But, Dad—!'

'Yes, dear, I know, but what else can we do? I suppose we might try asking him *politely*,' this with a twinkle at his daughter, 'but I don't suppose it will make any difference. Anyway, you said they won't start until the rain stops, and it doesn't look as though that will happen just yet. I should leave well alone and see what happens. Even if the rain stops they can't do much until the ground dries out. It isn't very good draining land, and they'll have to dig the footings well and deep, and they can't start that until the ground is much drier.'

'Why, Dad, how come you know so much about building?' Kestrel asked in surprise.

'Why shouldn't I know about building?' he asked with a smile. 'Did you think I was nothing but a cranky old bird-fancier?'

It was so close to the man's words—'bird crank'—that all Kestrel's love for her father welled up, and she flung her arms round him in a protective embrace.

'Oh, Dad, you're lovely.'

Mr Richards patted her shoulder affectionately, surprised and pleased by the burst of affection. 'Of course I am, my dear, I've been telling you that for years.'

Kestrel laughed, released him, sniffed away a tear, and smiled.

'Let's have a cup of tea,' she said.

CHAPTER 6

Anyone who relies on the English weather for anything is doomed to disappointment. Kestrel woke the next morning very early, and lay for a moment puzzled as to what it was that was out of the ordinary, what it was that had woken her up. Then she realised that it was the sun, shining in through her bedroom window.

She groaned aloud, climbed out of bed, and went to look out through the curtains. The sun was shining low over the marsh, lighting up every wet surface, and slowly climbing a sky that was cloudless and looked like staying that way.

'It would!' she said to herself. 'Of all the perverse—!' But it was a lovely morning for anything other than protecting the harriers, and she was not so insensitive to it that she could go back to bed. She washed and dressed hastily and went downstairs. She listened a moment for her father, decided he was still asleep, found a basket, and let herself out of the side door to go mushrooming.

She didn't expect to find many, it not being very good mushroom country, but it was a good excuse to get out in that still, white part of the early morning, before anyone is around to use the day up and smudge its beauty. She walked up to Dodman's and then leaving the road, which performed a loop towards the village, she climbed over a wall into a field opposite and wandered along beside the hedge, cutting off the loop and finding one or two firm white mushrooms for her trouble.

She took a meandering way through the fields, never far from the village though never right in it, and at last, finding that she was hungry and that her feet, clad in plimsolls, were cold from the dew, she worked her way back to the road, intending to head for home. She got back onto the road by cutting through Miss O'Connor's garden, which brought her into the village just above the Bell.

The last person she expected to see

73

out that early was the last person she wanted to see, but as she was about to leave the garden by the gate she saw, coming towards her down the road, a tall figure in a raincoat. She drew back into the shadow of the hedge before he saw her, and immediately wondered why she had—it was ridiculous to try to avoid him. Since she had, however, she stayed where she was and watched him. He was obviously going back to the hotel after an early walk. She wouldn't have expected him to be the kind who got up early.

Perhaps he had been to the site? But no, he was coming from the other direction. He passed her hiding-place without noticing her, and she had a close-up view of his (she had to admit it) rather handsome profile. His face was serious, almost sad. She thought what an incongruous figure he made in the village street in his new, clean raincoat—and perhaps a rather lonely figure? She shook herself. Why should she feel sorry for him? He would probably take it as a great insult if he knew.

When he was safely out of sight, Kestrel emerged from her hedge and made her way home. The morning was beginning to be peopled, and she passed the postman on his way back from Coats Cottage, and when she reached Dodman's Corner, old Mr Ambrose was out in his garden, snuffing the air like an old grey terrier.

'Ah, mornin' Miss Castrol,' he said, giving her a most unearthly knowing wink. 'Been out mushroomin' I see. Didjer meet up with that young feller while you was out, hey?'

'What young feller?' Kestrel asked irritably.

'Oh, he's a grand young man, that one,' Mr Ambrose went on, ignoring Kestrel's question, as well he might. 'Looks proper smart, like as he might be well off. Nice lookin' too,' he added musingly, 'if that's anythin' to go by. But you'd know more about that than an old man like me, wouldn't you, hey?'

'I really don't know him at all,' Kestrel said distantly, 'and I've only spoken to him once.' She meant to give the impression that if she never spoke to him again it would be too soon, but Mr Ambrose gave her a toothless grin and took it the other way.

'Well, don't you mind it,' he said. 'He'll be here for a long while yet, so you'll have your chance.'

'I must go—Dad'll be waiting for his

breakfast,' she said hastily, and made her escape.

After breakfast her father set off for the nest site. 'I'm building a rough hide on the other side from the building site,' he said. 'If I'm going to be watching the birds seriously I must at least be able to sit on something dry. I'm not as young as I was,' he told Kestrel.

'Well, I'll just do the washing up and tidy up a bit,' she said, 'and then I'll follow.'

'I'd be grateful if you'd come via the village and get me a ball of green twine,' her father said. 'I've only about half a yard left.'

'Okay, Dad,' she said resignedly, for she had hoped to avoid the village for the day. 'I'll see you later then.'

The sun was still shining strongly as she walked into the village, and there was a fresh little drying breeze. Monday's washing was up on lines in every garden, flapping with wet cracks and glittering in the sun, and the garden hedges were strewn with handkerchiefs, in places so thickly that it looked like a snow-fall. There were clouds in the dark blue sky, great white cumulous clouds, and Kestrel peered upwards, hoping to see some sign of rain in them, but they weren't that kind of cloud.

Mr Barrow was in the hardware and general store buying pea-sticks when Kestrel went in for the twine. He looked round at her and his eye lit up.

'Morning, Kestrel—I've just seen that young man go past, only a minute ago,' he said. Kestrel smiled wearily.

'Oh, have you?' she said without interest. 'Do you think it'll rain again?'

'No,' he said, successfully diverted, for, like all the villagers, he thought himself an expert on meteorology. 'No, I reckon it's set fair for a while. Time too—else all me veg'll rot in the ground. Terrible lot er wet this time a year—do for the onions and potatoes, you see if it don't. Still, it do look set fair for a bit.'

'Good drying wind, too,' said Jim Cosser, the owner of the store. 'See all the washing out—that's a sight I've not seen for a week or two. Anything else for you, Arnie?' he added, seeing Kestrel fidget.

'No, that's all, Jim. Be seeing you—cheerio, Kestrel. Give my regards to your young man.' And he made his exit cackling, very pleased with himself.

After all the talk, she was prepared for the sight of the young man on the building site, but in fact he was not to be seen. There was plenty of activity, though, for besides Bill Partridge there was a middle-aged man in a cap and two other youths, obviously Cossey's men, for they were not villagers. They were laying down a board walk over the wet ground, and a load of timber had been delivered and was waiting to be stacked. As she made her way round the dry edge of the site Bill saw her and came across to speak to her.

He looked apologetic. 'I'm sorry,' he said. 'Mr King's been here this morning, and he wants things moving. Very sharp man, he seems to be.'

'That's the agent, is it? I didn't know his name.'

'Stuart King,' Bill told her. 'Them others is the foreman and two blokes from Cossey's—Lowestoft men. I spoke to the foreman once Mr King had gone, but he's a bit of a tartar. He said Mr King'd be on his tail if he was to mess about for a—something—bird. Beg pardon, but he was quite sharp.'

Kestrel looked down. 'You did your best, Bill. I suppose the foreman has to

78

do what he's told. No, it'll be this King bloke I'll have to get after.'

'Maybe it'll rain again,' Bill said after a short silence. Kestrel looked up at the sky and shook her head.

'Maybe. I'll have to hope so. Seen my father?'

'I did catch sight of him a while back, but since then I haven't been looking. Gaffer keeps us up to the mark—there, he's looking at me now. I'll have to go.'

'Yes, you go on—I don't want to get you into trouble. Thanks for trying, Bill.'

He made a vague gesture of his hand and stumped off through the mud. It still looked pretty sloppy, she thought with relief. Then she went to find her father. He was working at his own gentle pace on the hide, and took the twine from her without comment. He moved so quietly and easily that he seemed a part of the wild, and it moved round him undisturbed as if he were no more than a fieldmouse. Kestrel was vaguely surprised to see Larch there, moving in and out of the tussocks on some business or game of his own. He greeted her with a quiet 'prrp' and a flashing glance from his sapphire eyes.

'Is he being a nuisance?' Kestrel asked

her father. He glanced down at the cat and smiled. Larch smiled back.

'Oh no—he's one of us, I think.'

'Are they still there?' She hardly dared ask this, though she knew they must be, or he would not still be calmly building like this.

'Yes—they don't seem to be too troubled yet, I'm glad to say. They stop rather more frequently to look around them—but so far that's the only sign of disturbance. There are, after all, only three men, and their presence is intermittent.'

'But if the activity increases—?'

'The building activity? Yes, that would make a difference. And if they bring any kind of machinery in—' He didn't finish the sentence.

'They're bound to, sooner or later, unless we can do something,' Kestrel began, but her father put up a hand to silence her, and his binoculars were at his eyes so quickly she didn't see the movement. Kestrel stiffened, and glancing down saw Larch at her feet, also frozen and staring through a gap at the bottom of the branches Mr Richards had already put together. Was it possible that the cat really *was* bird watching? And then she saw the harriers.

When they had gone and the three of them unfroze, she asked,

'What were they carrying? Are they still building?'

'It appears so, I'm very glad to say,' her father answered, and Kestrel smiled with relief.

Towards lunchtime the harriers disappeared, so Mr Richards decided to go back home for a bite to eat and to write up some notes, and then come back in the evening.

'What will you do?' he asked his daughter.

'I think I'll go and have lunch with Theo,' she said. 'She may have some ideas about what we might do.'

'Yes, she might indeed. She strikes me as a young lady of a very practical turn.'

'And she likes birds,' Kestrel smiled. Her father smiled back.

'Do you know, that's the first time you've smiled this morning,' he said teasingly. 'Keep it up—it might become a habit.'

As she picked her way back across the building site, she saw that Stuart King was back on site. Stuart King—it seemed strange to know his name. It suited him—a cold, haughty name, a

81

sophisticated, heartless name. He looked across at her as she passed near him, and she pretended to ignore him. Then his eye moved a little behind her, and he began to laugh. Kestrel glanced quickly back and saw that Larch was behind her, walking in her wake as a dog might. The big cat stopped as she stopped and gave her a silent miaou. It really was rather funny, but she didn't like *that man* laughing at her, and with reddening cheeks she put her head up and marched on without another glance.

Larch was still with her when she reached the library, and she stopped and looked down at him, wondering whether to take him inside to Laura. But at that moment, as if the meeting had been prearranged, the library door opened and Laura came out.

'Ah, there you are,' she said by way of greeting. 'Hello, cat. Where have you been?'

'Bird-watching again, if you can believe it. You know, I really do think he does watch them. He was prowling around Dad's hide, but when the harriers came he took up position where he could get a good view, and stayed quite still until they'd gone.'

Laura laughed. 'Nothing anyone tells me about any Siamese surprises me any more. They're more like people than people. Where are you off to, anyway?'

'I was just going to cadge some lunch from Theo.'

'Snap. So was I,' Laura said. 'Let's hope she did her shopping. Oh, by the way, your young man came into the library this morning.'

Kestrel's face darkened. 'If you're referring to the guest at the Bell, I'd be glad if you wouldn't refer to him as my young man.'

'Whoops!' Laura said with a comical face. 'Sorry, pardon. Why so savage, fair maid?'

'Everywhere I go in the village people keep telling me where he is and what he's doing—as if I care,' Kestrel glowered. 'I know any time an unmarried man comes within ten miles of Wesslingham everyone waits with baited breath to see if he'll marry me, but I'm getting a bit tired of it. And considering who this particular specimen is, I think it's rather tactless.'

'Consider it unsaid,' Laura said, but there was the suspicion of a grin lurking about her mouth that Kestrel didn't like the look of.

Theo was glad to see them as always, and was not unwilling to provide them with lunch. 'As long as you don't mind it being soup and cheese.'

'That's fine with me,' Kestrel said, sitting down and glancing round for the cat. 'Where's Larch?'

'He trotted off home,' Laura said. 'Left us when we passed our lane.'

'Oh, by the way,' Theo said, 'your young man was in here today, Kestrel. Took a very intelligent interest in some of my water-colours. I think he may have rather good taste.' Laura, who had been watching the thunderclouds gather on Kestrel's face, interrupted at that point.

'She doesn't like to have him mentioned, Theo, and particularly in that way. She took my head off for telling her he'd been in to the library this morning.'

'Oh, really? What did he come to the library for?' Theo asked.

'For a piano lesson, you idiot,' Laura said pleasantly. 'What do you think? He asked me if he could join, so I enrolled him as a temporary member, and he took out two books.' She gazed thoughtfully into the distance. 'He struck me as being rather a lonely type. He said he wanted something to read during the long evenings. Fair pulled at the old heart-strings.'

'Well, there isn't much to do in Wesslingham for a stranger,' Theo said sympathetically. 'Especially if you don't know anyone—and I don't suppose he wants to sit in with the Partridges every night.'

'Mm. Nice people, but not stirring company. And working with Bill during the day he'd probably be embarrassed to spend his leisure hours with him. I suppose he'll just go to his room and read. Sad really.'

'Is he married?' Theo asked.

'According to Mrs D he isn't, though I don't know how reliable that may be. He doesn't look married.'

Kestrel who had borne all this in silence so far, said crossly, 'How on earth can you tell from a person's looks if they're married or not?'

'Oh, I don't know. You just can,' Laura said. Her eye twinkled dangerously. Kestrel knew what she was thinking.

'What books did he take out?' she asked in spite of herself.

'A Patricia Highsmith and a P.G Wodehouse,' Laura said.

'Hmm,' Theo mused. 'Highbrow mystery and comedy. Not very revealing. But nothing you could hold against him, Kestrel.'

'Oh, shush!' she said, laughing at last. 'All right, so I'm interested in him—but not in that way. I just want to know what he's like so I can work out the best way of tackling him.'

'Over this bird business, you mean?' Theo asked.

'I think you're flogging a dead horse,' Laura said briskly. 'I don't see how the interests of one bird can weigh against an entire building firm. And presumably the local council gave planning permission, so I don't see that you've a leg to stand on.'

'You think it's just another bird, don't you,' Kestrel said. Laura shrugged.

'You can't halt progress, Kestrel. And think of the homeless people in the country. At least this lot are building houses, and not office blocks or roads.'

'But why here?' Theo came into the

argument. 'And for whom? The homeless of the land aren't going to be living in these houses. These are country houses for rich executives–Georgian-style residences, isn't that what they call them? We don't need the houses, and no working people could live in them, even if they were reasonably priced, because there's no work in these parts. People have to live near their work.'

'And look at those new houses they built over near Oulton Broad—they are still empty, though they were finished over a year ago,' Kestrel said. Laura lifted her hands.

'All right. I admit all that. But I still think you're flogging a dead horse. And he isn't going to listen to you anyway.'

'That's only too true,' Kestrel said gloomily. 'He thinks I'm a muddy hoyden—a bird freak, I think it was he called me.'

Theo laughed. 'Try not to mix personal pique with your crusading zeal,' she said. Kestrel stuck out her tongue, which was not elegant, but certainly forceful.

'How about this lunch?' Laura brought the argument to an end. 'I have to get back to work by a quarter to one.'

CHAPTER 7

When Kestrel arrived back home after lunch she found that her father had shut himself into his study with his notes, so she decided to occupy her afternoon doing the washing. It wasn't that they made much dirty between them, but as it was a job Kestrel hated, and as Mr Richards rarely remembered the existence of housework of any kind, it tended to build up until neither of them had anything at all to wear.

Might as well make use of this blasted weather, she thought, and accordingly wheeled out the washing machine, filled it, and threw in the first load of shirts and tee-shirts. As she sorted through the washing basket for the second load, it occurred to her just how limited her wardrobe really was, seeming to consist almost entirely of plain skirts, white blouses, and tee-shirts. 'Like a schoolgirl,' she said aloud. She remembered her own words—he thinks I'm a muddy hoyden. Why had this man got under her skin so? She had always dressed the same, never cared much for her appearance, so why should a stranger from Norwich affect her so deeply? Why should she care what he thought of her?

She tried to convince herself it was because of the danger to the harriers, but the memory of his stern profile came back to her from her morning's walk. Laura thinks he's lonely, she thought. She remembered that she had thought the same thing about him, seeing him returning from his solitary stroll. Well, anyone'd be lonely in a strange village. But that wasn't true—she, for instance, wouldn't be lonely in a strange village, because she'd jolly well go and *make* friends.

So why didn't he? It brought her back to her original idea about him, that he was simply too stuck-up to care for ordinary country people. Too proud and sophisticated to mix with them—the kind of man who stays in the best suite at the Bell. And I bet he goes out to Vernon's restaurant in the evening, or to the Crown at Southwick—that kind of place. He probably can't eat anything with an English name. I suppose he's got a car—I never thought to ask. Must see if Bill knows—I bet it's a posh one.

So her thoughts ran on while she did the washing and pegged it out in the afternoon sunshine. When she had finished, she found she still had time on her hands, and so she took the opportunity to go upstairs for a bath. In the bathroom she stripped off thoughtfully, and then took stock of herself in the bathroom mirror.

Hair—good and thick, and nicely curly, good colour too, but a general bird's-nest appearance and no style that was ever seen between two magazine covers. Face—she had lived with her face too long to see it as anything other than her face, and a fairly agreeable one, but now she had to admit that there was something unsophisticated about it. Her eyebrows were thick and dark, not faint, thin, arched lines the way models wore them; her nose was straight enough, but rather freckled, and with the faintest suggestion of a tilt at the end; her mouth was rather too wide; her skin was brown and her cheeks red, like a real country bumpkin—sophisticated girls were pale ivory all over.

Then there was the problem of her hands. She blushed faintly as she looked at them. She hadn't really considered them a problem before, but studying them now she realised that even the least fastidious of boyfriends wouldn't make them a subject of poetry. They were large and square, rough-skinned from work in the house and garden (she never could be bothered with rubber gloves); the forefinger of each had a line of ingrained dirt along it, and her fingernails, which she always kept cut short for convenience, were all odd lengths where they kept breaking in the course of her strenuous life.

Well, the hands at least she could do something about, she thought, and jumping into the bath she took the nail brush and the pumice stone to them. 'And afterwards,' she addressed them severely, 'I'll simply drown you in handcream—if I've got any.' At least she wouldn't be ashamed to shake hands with him after this.

Stuart King was finding Wesslingham less of a trial than he expected. True the job was well behind, but already the weather had changed for the better, and the men he had to work with seemed to be straight enough, and although slow workers, reasonably thorough. The villagers all seemed very friendly, and there was a very nice sympathetic lady in the local library with whom he had had quite a chat.

As far as his social life went, the one problem seemed to be that everyone wanted to pair him off with the Wild Woman of Borneo. He had not twigged it at first, why everyone mentioned her to him every time they met him—he had thought at first they somehow knew about her visit to the site and were simply making mischief. But after a while, the particular quality of their knowing winks or earnest speeches about her virtues—according to the character of the person who waylaid him, made him realise that it was matrimony that loomed large in their minds.

It bothered him more than a little. Apart from the fact that the Wild Woman was obviously all set to hate him to the hilt, she appeared to him to be only about seventeen, and he had never been that much of a baby-snatcher. If, as it appeared, she was the only unmarried girl in the village, he could understand their fixing their attention on her, but she was so young that he felt their concern over her spinsterhood was rather overdone.

Fortunately, he knew how to avoid her, in the evenings at least. One old boy had told him, laying considerable stress on it, that she had been in the Dog and Duck on Sunday night, so presumably that was where she took her cider, or whatever locals drank. So all he had to do was stay on his own ground, in the Bell, and he'd be safe. Well, safe from her at least.

Having spent all afternoon thinking about Stuart King, Kestrel decided it would all be wasted unless she used it in another attempt on his rigid mind, and so after tea she told her father that she would go in to the Bell for a drink, and went upstairs to change out of her jeans. She didn't want her appearance to look like an effort, but on the other hand she wanted at least to look as though she had chosen her clothes rather than been thrown into them.

After much more thought than the occasion merited, she chose a dark brown suede skirt, which, though old, had once been smart, and a pretty canary-yellow jumper. She wrestled her thick hair into the style she had worn it to work in town, which was with the front part drawn back into a knot and the back part hanging loose. It suited her quite well, and made her look older.

The main problem was what to wear on her feet. It was still very muddy down their lane, so the only sensible thing to wear was wellingtons; but that of course would spoil the effect of the skirt. She pondered on this for some time, and was almost ready to cry to hell with Stuart King and go in wellingtons anyway, when she remembered her father's bicycle. With the saddle right down she could manage that, and it would keep her well enough above the mud for her to wear shoes. She smiled happily at the solving of her problem, and put on, with pleasure and pride, her well-polished golf-style shoes.

'And that,' she said to her reflection, 'is good enough for Mr Stuart flaming King, even if he was from London itself.'

Her father obligingly lowered the saddle of the bike for her, and said he might come down later himself.

'Oh do, Dad, it would be lovely. It's months since we had a drink together.'

'Well, I'll see. Won't it make a problem of transport for coming back, though?'

'Oh no, you can give me a crossbar—or

94

I can walk even. It won't matter coming back if I get a bit muddy.'

Her father grinned at her suddenly. 'One of the things about you that I love, Kestrel, is your complete disregard of feminine wiles.'

If only you knew, Kestrel thought guiltily, and kissed him goodbye.

The bike idea worked quite well. She avoided the sloppiest parts of their lane, and although she got one or two dobs of mud on her legs, they were dry enough to scrape off, and her stockings were a dark colour anyway. She cycled along happily, humming a song, and thinking about nothing in particular, and, accustomed to the quietness of the lanes thereabouts, turned straight out of Coats Lane at Dodman's Corner without even looking. At once there was a blare of a car's horn and a squeal of brakes almost on top of her. She jerked her head round in alarm and twisted the handlebars sharply to avoid the car, wobbled frantically for a moment, and then went into the ditch.

It was a muddy ditch. She fell off sideways and the bike fell on top of her, smearing the oil from its unguarded chain onto her unguarded legs. The car—a mustard-yellow Capri—stopped a few yards further on, and for a moment or two there was no sound in the lane but the decelerating whirr of the bike's back wheel spinning in the ditch.

'I say, are you all right?' came a voice, and Kestrel, looking up from her muddy nest, saw the immaculate head of Stuart King framed against the sky.

'You!' she said in exasperation, and began, to her own surprise, to cry. 'Of course I'm not all right,' she sobbed. 'I'm covered in mud and oil. My clothes are ruined! It's no thanks to you I'm not dead.'

Stuart King had got out of his car with his knees shaking, ready to be apologetic, conciliatory, sympathetic or helpful as the occasion demanded, but this outburst from the person he had been congratulating himself on avoiding was too much. His manners held out, however, and he only said,

'It wasn't my fault, you know. You came straight out without looking.'

'You had no right to be travelling that fast on a road like this,' she said stormily. 'There could have been anything ahead of you—cows or children or anything—'

96

'Instead there was you,' he said, with an attempt at humour.

'Who else would you expect to be coming out of our lane?' Her tears were giving way before her anger now. He said,

'Well, do stop crying, anyway. You shouldn't really be riding a bike like this anyway—it's too big for you.'

'Don't talk to me like a child!' she shouted at him. 'And get this thing off me!'

He almost smiled, for sitting there in the ditch with her hair round her shoulders and her face smeared with mud and tears, she looked no more than thirteen, but he knew that young girls hated to have their age referred to, and he tactfully straightened his face and lifted the bike out onto the road.

'No damage done,' he said, having examined it for bent spokes. 'I expect your father will be glad—or is it your brother's?'

'No damage—I like that! What about my clothes? And my stockings are ruined,' she discovered. 'You really are a clumsy fool. Well, don't just stand there—help me up, can't you?'

'It was your own fault entirely,' he said, extending a hand and taking hers. 'I wasn't travelling too fast, and even if you've lived here all your life you should still look before you turn out of a side lane onto a bigger road. *You* didn't know what was there either.'

'Oh, shut up,' she said crossly, no longer able to think of anything clever to say. She was halfway to her feet at that point, and to her horror his hand somehow slipped out of hers and she went back into the mud with a resounding smack. She stared up at him in amazement.

'You did that deliberately,' she said, stunned by his behaviour.

'You deserved it. I don't see why I should help you if you're going to be rude to me.'

They looked at each other for a moment in silence, and then she began to cry again. It was not tears of temper this time, but tears of humiliation at this dismal end to her plan, and Stuart King watched her in growing concern, and regretted immediately his impulse of the moment.

'Hey, listen, I'm sorry—that was rotten of me,' he said at once. 'It was just that I—oh look, please don't cry. I *am* sorry.

I expect the mud will brush off when it's dry. Here, let me help you out—' and he reached out his hand for her again. She held out hers without looking, and as he leaned over to take it, he found her surprisingly strong fingers curling round his wrist and, with a quick jerk, she pulled him down into the ditch beside her.

'Why you—!' he glared at her tear-stained face. 'You were only pretending to cry.'

'I wasn't,' she hiccuped, not sure if she was laughing or crying, 'but you deserved it. You shouldn't be so damned patronising.'

'Of all the spoilt little brats I've ever met—'

'I should like to push your pompous face right into the mud,' Kestrel said fiercely. 'What do you mean by talking to me like that? I'm not a child, and I should have thought having thrown me into the ditch in the first place you would at least have the decency to help me out without patronising me. But then that's like you stuck-up city people—you think yourselves above it all. I expect you'll offer to pay for the cleaning and think that makes it all right.'

'I was going to offer to pay for the

cleaning, as a matter of fact,' he began, but broke off at the sight of her satisfied expression. 'So that's what you think of me...' he mused.

'Yes, and you needn't tell me what you think of me, because *that* has been evident from the first moment you saw me,' she said sharply. Stuart thought he caught a glimpse of some kind of pique behind those words, and as for a moment he studied her face, looking for clues, he saw her begin to blush. She turned her face away and put her hand up to it, feeling for mud smears.

'Every time you see me, I'm covered in mud,' she said, and he heard the tears of frustration not far behind her voice. He thought just then how superbly beautiful she would look dressed up to kill, and had Kestrel turned round at that moment and given him the full benefit of her deep blue eyes, he might well have found himself very vulnerable. What did happen, however, was that a high cackling laugh from above them diverted their attention, and they saw Mr Ambrose doubled up with laughter, slapping his knee with delight at the sight of the two of them sitting in the mud.

'Oh, this is a sight for sore eyes!' he

chortled. 'What a crying shame to see you all muddy, Miss Castrol, and your pretty clothes all a-muddy, but oh, you do look a precious sight, you do, and the gent from Norwich too. Oh, I shall remember this a many a long day, I shall!'

He shook his head, wiped a tear from the corner of his eye, and shuffled back across the road to take up his favourite watching position at his own gate.

Subdued, Stuart clambered out of the mud and helped Kestrel out, this time without mishap. They surveyed each other soberly.

'You realise this will be all over the village by tomorrow, and not the true version either,' Kestrel said. He nodded, and chewed his lip.

'Listen, I am sorry about your clothes— such a pretty colour too, that jumper. I wish there was something I could do to make it up to you.'

'Oh, it doesn't matter,' Kestrel began, and then changed her mind, and went on, 'about the clothes—but you can make it up to me. You can stop the building on that site.'

Stuart's face, which had been open with sympathy, closed against her, and his voice was cold as he replied.

'Now I'm afraid you're being frivolous. You know that isn't possible.'

'I don't know anything of the sort,' she began passionately, but he interrupted her.

'I really don't want to talk about that, especially with you, here, and in this condition. If you are all right, I think you should get home and have a hot bath or something. If you'd like to send me the cleaning bill, I'll pay it of course.'

'Quite the gentleman,' Kestrel spat, and then bit her lip. She really hadn't meant to be rude, but something about his tone of voice set her off, and she saw at once she had offended him. Before she could say she was sorry, he had turned on his heel and walked off towards his car without another word.

CHAPTER 8

Mr Richards was sympathetic, but not so much so that he couldn't see that it had been her fault in the main.

'I suppose we all get too blasé about

the roads,' he said, 'but it doesn't make it any better that we all do it. I'm just glad nobody was hurt.'

'Except my pride,' Kestrel said ruefully. Now that she was at home and changed into her comfortable jeans, she was beginning to see the funny side. 'And also, whatever chance there was of getting him on our side, it must be all out of the window now. He'll never forgive me for pulling him in after me.'

'I'm sorry to have to say it, but I wish I'd been there to see it,' Mr Richards said, a smile pulling at the corner of his mouth.

'Old Mr Ambrose was,' Kestrel told him. 'He came all the way across the road on purpose to tell me that he'd never forget it as long as he lived. It'll be all over the village tomorrow.'

'Ah well, that can't be helped. It will just enhance your reputation a little more.'

'What reputation?' Kestrel asked.

'Your reputation for being unmarriage-able,' Mr Richards said, his eyes twinkling. 'No-one would marry a woman with your temper, now would they?'

'I wish I could be sure,' Kestrel said gloomily. 'Sure that's what they'll think, I mean. I have the feeling they'll take it as being a sign from heaven that this man and I are made for each other, or some such tripe, and they'll matchmake all the harder.'

'My darling girl, you ought to be used to it by now—and it's done in kindness of heart, you know.'

'Oh, I know, but it's a bit wearing, that's all. Shall we put our boots on and tramp across the marsh and drop in at the Dog and Duck on our way back for a half-pint?'

Mr Richards put his arm around her shoulders and kissed the top of her head.

'What a good idea,' he said. 'And you did look pretty tonight, before your mud-bath, in case nobody thought to tell you.'

'Nobody did—but thank you. I think I shall confine myself to looking pretty for you from now on. They say pride goeth before a fall.'

'You always look pretty to me,' said her father, and his voice had the ring of truth. In complete harmony with each other they took their walk in the gathering dark across the marsh they knew so well, and by the time they reached the Dog and Duck it was quite dark, and the lights of the pub shone out through the low casements in a most welcoming way.

They scraped the mud off their boots on the cast-iron scraper that stood at the door for that purpose, and went in out of the slight chill to the inn parlour. As she came through the door, Kestrel was not surprised to hear Joe Lambert greet her with a cheerful sally.

'Hello, Kestrel. Well, I've heard of ladies using mudpacks, but I didn't know they was applied to *that* end of you.' His gesture was indescribably comic, and Kestrel, despite her resolutions, couldn't help joining in the laugh.

There was nothing to laugh at the next day, however. The day dawned fine again, and both Kestrel and her father were out early. Armed with their usual gear—binoculars and notebook—they walked down to the hide and took up their position to watch the harriers. They were both out hunting, sweeping low across the marshes and uttering their plaintive cry, and occasionally disappearing from the watchers' view into some cover, presumably to eat what they had caught.

It was at half past seven that the trouble started, for that was when the men arrived on the building site, and they arrived in a Bedford van only shortly before a dump truck and a cement mixer. Kestrel and her father exchanged anxious glances, but there was nothing they could do but watch.

'I wouldn't have thought the ground was dry enough yet,' Kestrel said to her father, subconsciously hoping that his opinion would make the thing fact, but he only shrugged.

'I don't know. Perhaps they have just brought it along for future use. Perhaps they won't use it today.'

From the moment the men arrived the birds had shown their uneasiness. They flew back and forth near the nest site, calling to each other, making short, nervous flights unlike their former sweeping grace. At first they continually flew back to the nest site, perching near it and looking around with quick movements of the head, but gradually they moved further from it, their flights taking them steadily away from the movement and noise on the site.

The female seemed more willing to stay than the male, but when the first engine started up, her own courage gave out, and with a cry of alarm she flew off to where the male was waiting for her, some distance away. For a moment they sat side by side, alert, and then they took off, flying away towards the sea.

'Oh Dad!' Kestrel cried, almost in tears. 'They've gone. Oh, the beasts, how can they be so noisy? I've a good mind to go in there and break their wretched machine.'

'For heaven's sake, Kestrel!' Mr Richards was alarmed. 'Don't let this action-woman reputation of yours go to your head. That kind of thing is criminal damage—you could get into very serious trouble. I know you don't mean it, but don't even say it.'

'I do mean it!' she said fiercely, her fists clenched. 'If that's the only way to stop them, I'll do it—put sugar in the petrol tank or something. The birds are more important than their smelly, stinking, clattering machine.'

'I absolutely forbid you to do anything of the sort. In fact,' he went on seriously, 'It would be better if you didn't go anywhere near the building site.

'Why? Why shouldn't I go across it as I always do?'

'Because, child, if there was any sort of accidental damage done and it was known that you had been there, and that you had a grudge against them, it might look very much as though you had done it.'

She thought for a minute. 'Do you mean that he'd go so far as to *frame* me?' Her father sighed.

'No, I don't mean that. Why must you make everything so dramatic? It must be the influence of all that television you watch.'

'Darling, Dad,' Kestrel smiled, squeezing his arm, 'you know I hardly ever watch it, except for the wild-life programmes. I suppose I am being dramatic, but I can't help it. That man brings out the worst in me.'

'Oh, I don't know—you look rather nice when you're angry,' her father said. 'And now, don't you think we had better go and try to find the harriers?'

Kestrel had forgotten them momentarily, and her face grew suddenly grave as the memory returned.

'Oh gosh, yes—how terrible of me to let them out of my mind for a minute.'

'It's only to be expected—you are young, you've more things to think about than mere birds.'

'Dad!'

'I'm teasing you, child. Come on, we

108

must move. I'd like to know where they are. I might be able to gather something from their movements. They may have been only temporarily startled. I certainly hope so. It would be a tragedy if we've seen the last of our nesting pair.'

The morning wore on, but they did not catch a glimpse of the two birds, and Kestrel's spirits sank. Her father, seeing this, suggested they split up to cover two separate areas, and meet again at lunchtime to compare notes.

'We've a better chance of finding them if we cover a larger area,' he said.

'Of course,' Kestrel agreed. 'Who's to have the bins?'

'There's a spare pair in my haversack.' Kestrel reached in and found the small pocket binoculars he carried as spares.

'If you do spot them,' he told her, 'stay quiet and watch them carefully so that you can tell me exactly what they're doing. And don't worry—I don't think they've been scared right off.'

'Yet,' Kestrel added, and he didn't refute the word.

They parted and trudged off in opposite directions. Kestrel noted that the cloud that had been low on the horizon that morning was coming up rapidly from seaward, and that the wind was freshening. It was from the north-east, a wind that usually brought rain, and by the time she decided to head back for lunch the sky was completely overcast and the first few spots were falling.

'Perhaps it will hold up the building,' she thought. 'Oh I *do* hope so—and I hope it isn't too late. I wonder if Dad's found them yet? I think I'll walk back by the building site and see if they mind the rain.'

It was quite a long walk back, and by the time she got there the rain was falling steadily from an iron-grey sky, and the building site was indeed deserted. Her heart rose a little, and she surveyed the sky anxiously until she had satisfied herself that there wasn't a single break in the cloud cover anywhere. She turned her footsteps homewards, and as she neared the church she saw two figures standing, one either side of the churchyard wall, conversing—her father and the vicar, of course.

'I must say,' Mr Truman greeted her when she came up to them, 'I didn't think I'd see the day when I'd welcome this much rain, but it's happened. I could hardly believe it when the first few drops fell. I was in the church sorting out the music for choir-practice tonight when I heard it rattle against the windows. So I slipped out with my umbrella and went along to the—enemy camp, if I might put it that way.'

'You see he takes it as seriously as you do,' Mr Richards said to Kestrel.

'Oh indeed, indeed!' the vicar said earnestly. 'I cannot hope to have another chance of seeing a nesting pair of harriers practically on my own doorstep.'

'And what happened at the building site?' Kestrel prompted him.

'Oh, yes—well, by the time I got there it was raining in earnest, and the men stopped work and went and sat in the little hut for shelter. I suppose they were waiting to see if it would stop again, but after a while that young man—Mr King, isn't it?—came along and spoke to the older man—I believe he's the foreman—and he sent them off home.'

'Well, it must have been obvious even to him that this wouldn't stop soon,' Kestrel said with an edge to her voice that didn't escape the vicar.

'Poor man,' he said. 'I felt quite sorry for him—it is his job, after all, and it must be very frustrating for him to be held up by something over which he has no control.'

'I hope you didn't feel constrained to pray for fine weather on his behalf,' Mr Richards said drily.

'Oh no—when it comes to a choice between him and the harriers, I'm afraid he doesn't stand a chance. But why don't we all go into the vestry, out of the rain?'

'Well, I was just off home for some lunch,' Kestrel said, looking at her father, but he nodded to the vicar and said,

'No, we'll come in and talk for a minute. I was just telling Mr Truman, Kestrel, about our problem, and he suggested a campaign.'

'Campaign?'

'Yes, come in and talk about it.'

The vestry was dry and warm and fusty, like all vestries. The two visitors set themselves down on hard vestry chairs, while the vicar leaned elegantly against the cope chest.

'Did you see the birds, Dad?' was Kestrel's first question when she got the water out of her ears. Funny how one never noticed how wet one was until one got into the dry.

'Yes, in the distance. I didn't get very close to them, but they were at least hanging around the area and not heading for distant parts.'

'Where were they?' Kestrel asked anxiously.

'Over near Colmansfield, where that patch of still water is.'

'But that's so far away!' Kestrel cried.

'Not to a harrier,' her father said. 'But that was why I didn't get closer.'

'Will they come back?'

'I think so. They'll probably come back this evening, and when they see the place deserted it may calm their fears. I hope so, anyway. But that brings us to the problem—if the rain stops, the same thing will happen again, and there's a limit to how many times they'll come back.'

'There's also a limit to how long the rain can go on,' the vicar interposed at this point. 'That was why I suggested we get up a campaign to protect the birds.'

'A campaign in the village?' Kestrel said doubtfully.

'Initially, of course, we'll have to get the support of the village. The idea will be to get enough support to present a proposition at the next parish council meeting, which is next week. They would be able to put enough pressure on the developers to get them to hold off while we seek further advice.'

'It sounds terribly slow,' Kestrel said, privately resolving that if necessary she would still try two pounds of Tate & Lyle in the petrol tank, at least as a temporary measure.

'It seems to me the only way,' the vicar said. 'We should get the campaign under way at once, and hold a meeting in the village hall as soon as possible to get a vote on the motion.'

'A meeting when?' Kestrel asked.

'On Sunday I thought, Sunday evening, after evensong.'

'Sunday? Why not tonight? It may stop raining tomorrow.'

'We have to have time to publicise the meeting and do a bit of persuading, my dear,' Mr Richards said. 'We want a good turnout at the meeting, or the motion won't carry any weight.'

'And besides,' the vicar said, 'it will mean a captive audience of all those at evensong. I'll shepherd them along to the village hall myself.'

'Provided they don't defect as they pass the Bell,' Kestrel said.

'I'll see they don't,' said the vicar. 'And now, have you contacted the RSPB, I wonder? They ought to be able to give us some advice. Perhaps they would send someone along to address our meeting—a professional speaker is so much more impressive to the village audience than someone they know.'

'I did write to them as soon as I identified the bird,' Mr Richards said. 'In fact, I should think their reply is waiting at home for us now—we came out before the post this morning. But I shall certainly contact them again. I'll phone them this afternoon and ask about a speaker.'

'Good,' said the vicar. 'Well, I shall do a little door-to-door campaigning this afternoon—I have several visits on my list for today, and I can fit quite a few more in before choir-practice. I shall address the choir of course—and you'll both do your best to spread the word, won't you?'

'Of course,' said Mr Richards. 'I'll tell Mr Ambrose—that should ensure a good broadcasting.'

'And I'll go along and see Theo,' said

Kestrel with sudden inspiration, 'and ask her if she'll do some posters for us. A good bright poster in the post office window, and one in Cosser's, and one in the library—that should help our cause.'

'What a good idea,' Mr Truman said. 'You might get Joe Lambert to put one up in the bar of the Dog and Duck, too. I don't suppose Mr Partridge will want to show one in the Bell, since the Leader of the Opposition is actually staying there—one can't ask him to jeopardise his livelihood.'

But, Kestrel suddenly thought as she headed for Theo's shop through the now driving rain, that's what we expect Stuart King to do. The idea made her momentarily uncomfortable.

CHAPTER 9

The village street was deserted, and since the clouds had come down low and heavy it was almost as dark as twilight. It could be a lonely place in this kind of weather, Kestrel thought, if you didn't know that all the people who usually hung around outside the post office, and on the bench outside the public library, were inside their snug houses with the tea brewing.

The rain pelted suddenly, and she skipped down the street, hugging the walls for protection, and darted into Theo's shop, where she stood shaking the water out of her hair and eyes.

'I don't know why you don't get yourself a sou'wester,' Theo said by way of greeting. 'I'm sure it can't do your hair any good to get perpetually soaked like that.'

'It doesn't get perpetually soaked—only when it rains,' Kestrel said reasonably. 'And it's God's rain, after all.'

'Don't start that!' Theo groaned, coming forward to take Kestrel's anorak from her. 'I went into the post office this morning for some stamps and had twenty minutes of Mrs Dorrit on the rain. She seems to have a special licence from God, or something, to interpret His signs. I don't know what the vicar's going to do when she makes him redundant. According to her gospel, the rain's a judgement on the village for all the wickedness that went on last year under cover of the hot weather—women parading their bodies in bikinis and so on.'

Kestrel laughed. 'I didn't see much parading, except on the part of the holidaymakers—and then most of the bikinis were worn by children under ten. But talking of the vicar—'

'Who was? By the way, do you want some coffee?'

'When did I ever refuse?'

'Well, go through and sit down—take the chairs off the end table and we'll be comfortable about it. No-one will come to the shop in this rain.'

'Well, that's good, because I want to talk to you,' Kestrel said.

'Oh yes, about the vicar! Well, wait until I get the coffee on the table,' Theo answered. Kestrel sat down at one of the pretty pine tables in the back of the shop and switched on the light that hung low over the table top—it was really quite dark outside. Theo brought a pot of coffee to the table, and a luscious-looking coffee walnut gateau. 'A new recipe I'm trying out,' she said. 'You must tell me what you think of it.'

'It looks too good for the summer trade,' Kestrel said.

'What a cruel woman you can be,' Theo said, sitting down and pouring the coffee.

118

'Help yourself. Now, what has the vicar been doing?'

Kestrel told her about the disturbance of the birds that morning, and about Mr Truman's suggestion of a campaign. 'He's going to do door-to-door canvassing, and we're to have a big meeting in the village hall on Sunday after evensong to get support for a motion to go before the parish council next week. My only fear is that it won't be soon enough to do any good. If the rain stops the machines will start, and the birds will go.'

'And these kind of councils are so very slow and hide-bound,' Theo said thoughtfully, 'though of course this is the kind of motion that would appeal to them. And there are a lot of bird-fanciers amongst them—Colonel Drake and Mrs Humphries and that crowd.'

Kestrel nodded. 'But I've decided, if the worst comes to the worst, I'll try sabotage.'

Theo looked up sharply. 'You mean holing their wellies, that kind of thing?'

'Not quite,' Kestrel grinned. 'I won't say more for fear of incriminating you. But what I really came for was to enlist your support in the matter of posters—could

119

you knock us out something eyecatching to get people along to the meeting?'

'I deplore your language—"knock out", indeed, when referring to one of my masterpieces—but I'll certainly help. How many do you want?'

'About half a dozen, if you've time,' Kestrel said. 'One for the post office, of course, and one for the library—Laura will hang it in a prominent place—'

'Laura isn't keen on this bird business, you know,' Theo warned. 'She's terribly practical, and she doesn't think it's worth knocking your head against a brick wall.'

'But she isn't anti, is she?'

'No, not really, just not keen. Then there's her vegetables, of course. New people living in the new houses would mean customers for her. And she feels very sorry for the agent-wallah.'

Kestrel wasn't sure how serious Theo was—it was difficult to tell with her when she kept a straight face—but she answered in like vein. 'Well, you can tell her that the birds would make the village famous and she could make a fortune selling fruit and veg to the tourists. And as for Stuart King—'

'Yes? I'm interested to see how you're

going to do away with that objection.'

'How about this? If this building goes on, he'll get promoted for straightening out a difficult job, and he'll get sent out to supervise a building job in the desert for the Arabs and die of sunstroke. So she'd be doing him a favour not to support him.'

'Ingenious,' Theo laughed. 'But to be serious for a moment, I'm still wondering about this campaign—about whether it will have any effect, or enough effect.'

'You think we shouldn't do it?'

'Oh no, I think we should go ahead with it, but I think we need more pressure than that on the builders to make them give up the project when it's this far ahead. We need much wider support for the birds.'

'Newspapers?' Kestrel suggested. Theo shook her head.

'Wider still. Television. Specifically, the six o'clock magazine programme, *Roundabout*—or at least, the part of it that deals with East Anglia.'

'It *sounds* good, but how?' Kestrel asked.

'It just so happens that I know the editor of the programme rather well—Tony Flaxman's his name, and he and I worked together years ago on a similar kind of programme—'

121

'You worked for the BBC?' Kestrel broke in in surprise.

'I still do, on and off,' Theo said with becoming modesty. Kestrel's face overspread with a seraphic smile.

'So that's what you do on those mysterious trips into town. I *knew* it was something exciting, but I didn't know what. I'd put you down as a secret agent.'

'You do talk nonsense,' Theo smiled. 'Keep to the point. The thing is, I'm sure I could persuade Tony to do a bit on the harriers on the Anglia section of *Roundabout*. And one of his researchers ought to be able to find out who the people are behind the development and maybe put a bit of pressure on them.'

'The programme would certainly impress people round this part of the world,' Kestrel said eagerly. 'Practically everyone watches *Roundabout*, because of the farming news, and they take everything it says as gospel.' She thought for a minute. 'But when could it be done? If it isn't soon, it won't be any use. I expect his programme will be all booked up for weeks ahead.'

Theo laughed. 'That's not the way that kind of programme works. They have to be able to put in fresh news right up to the last minute, or the programme would be stale as old buns. No, don't worry—the speed is part of the charm. I'll go up and see him tomorrow morning, and I'm pretty sure I can persuade him to put it on right away—say on Friday night. Friday's the best night, because they have the extended local sections, and the biggest audience.'

'Friday! That would be tremendous!' Kestrel cried, feeling cheerful all at once. 'It'll make sure everyone comes to the meeting on Sunday, too, and it'll show Mr Stuart King we mean business—'

She broke off abruptly at those words, for at that moment the shop door opened, with a cheerful tinkling of the Chinese shop-bell Theo had fixed up, and the subject of the conversation came in. He paused just inside the door as if not sure he was in the right place, and Theo at once got up and went towards him.

'Hello! What can I do for you?' she said pleasantly. He looked rather pathetic at that moment, for his hair was plastered down on his head with the rain, and water dripped off the ends of it and down his neck. His smart white raincoat was no longer quite perfect, having mud splashes round the bottom, and his boots were no longer black and shiny, their former glory dimmed.

'I'm not sure if I've been told right,' he said in answer to Theo's query. 'I was asking around if there was anywhere in the village I could get a cup of coffee or something—it's so gloomy sitting in my room, and I don't like to trouble Mrs Partridge all the time—and they said in the post office that you run a kind of cafe here in the summer.'

'I do, but only in the summer,' Theo said. 'For the visitors, you know. It wouldn't pay to open in the winter.'

'Oh, I see,' he said, and there was indescribable disappointment in his voice. Kestrel, who was hidden from his sight by a large rubber plant, got a sudden vision of what it must be like to have nowhere to go and nothing to do on a day such as this.

'But as it happens,' Theo went on quickly, 'I've just made some coffee, and I've a coffee gateau I'm trying out the recipe for, so you're welcome to come in and join us.'

'I say, thanks a lot—that's very kind of you,' he began happily, and then, taking a step forward towards the lighted table, he saw who the other person present was. He stopped. 'Oh,' he said.

'Oh indeed,' Theo said. 'I believe you know Miss Kestrel Richards, daughter of our local and very illustrious ornithologist?'

'We have met,' he said awkwardly. Kestrel tried to look indifferent.

'Oh, don't let me put you off. It's a beast of a day for walking the streets.'

'That's very kind of you, but I don't want to butt in,' he said firmly.

'No, no, you're not butting in,' Theo said blandly. 'Sit down, take off your coat.'

'You don't understand—I'm afraid Miss Richards and I are—not quite strangers. I'm afraid my presence would be unwelcome,' he said very stiffly.

'I know all about the mud-bath incident,' Theo said, 'and all I can say is it proves there's nothing to choose between you for silliness. Now do sit down. If Kestrel objects she can always go—she's had her coffee.'

Kestrel laughed at that, and Stuart looked at her in surprise, thinking how different she looked when she was relaxed and not blazing with temper.

'If you're sure,' he said hesitantly. Kestrel took up the thread.

'Yes, do. You've as much right here as me. And anyway—I wanted to apologise for what I did the other day. You had your decent clothes on, and it was uncalled for.'

'Well, I'm sorry too—your clothes must have been ruined too,' he said, relieved at the chance to apologise.

'It was my fault—I wasn't watching where I was going,' Kestrel said.

'It was my fault too—I shouldn't have been going so fast,' Stuart went on.

'Oh, for heaven's sake shut up, both of you,' Theo said pleasantly. 'This could go on for ever. How do you like your coffee?'

'Black please, and no sugar,' Stuart said. Theo smiled. 'A man of taste,' she said, throwing the ghost of a wink at Kestrel, who glared back. Then Theo went into the kitchen at the back to fetch more coffee, and Stuart and Kestrel found themselves unexpectedly alone. There was an awkward silence.

'Terrible weather,' he said at last, to break it.

'For you it is,' Kestrel said. He did not pick up the significance of this and went on,

126

'Yes—we've had to call off work for the day. I don't think it's going to stop before this evening.'

'My birds have had to call off building too,' Kestrel said, striving to keep her voice even. 'They were driven away this morning by the noise.'

'I'm sorry,' he said awkwardly.

'Are you?'

'Sorry for you, because I can see that the birds are important to you,' he said, trying to be fair. 'But it can't be helped. The houses must go up—they're needed.'

'Who by?' Kestrel said. 'They aren't council houses for poor people living in slums, or for the homeless. They're expensive houses for rich people. How are they needed? How are they going to help the housing situation?' Her voice began to take on an edge, and it needled Stuart.

'That's a very naïve way to look at it,' he said. 'The people who buy these houses will sell their present, cheaper houses. Other people will buy those and sell their present, even cheaper houses. And so on. The process runs right through, eventually releasing the cheapest type of housing for the first-time buyers. *That's* how it helps the homeless. And remember, with the cost of labour and materials at the moment it's almost impossible to build a new house cheap enough for the first-time buyer.'

'That sounds all very well, but the fact remains there are lots of houses like the ones you're trying to build still empty, and there are very few of the cheapest sort—and a lot of them are falling down.'

Stuart opened his mouth to reply, and changed his mind. 'There's no point in this kind of argument when only one of us knows the facts,' he said.

'The facts about what? You may know the facts about building, but what do you know about birds?'

'As little as I need to know. Birds simply aren't important.'

'So you think man is the only creature with a right to live on this planet, do you?' Kestrel said hotly, and at that moment Theo came back in with the coffee-pot.

'Coffee!' she trilled. 'Do I hear the silver tones of raised voices? Can't I leave you for a minute without you arguing?'

'I was trying not to,' Stuart said, 'but—'

'But you're too much of a gentleman to blame the lady for provoking you,' Theo finished for him. He grinned unwillingly and looked across at Kestrel. Their eyes met, and for a strange moment she felt oddly akin to him, as if they had known each other all their lives, as if they had grown up together, as if she and he... But it lasted only the briefest moment, and it made no sense anyway.

'It seems we're both immovable,' she said firmly, her cheeks crimsoning with confusion. She slid her eyes away from his, and said defiantly, 'But I'm not beaten. I won't be beaten.'

'Of course you won't,' Theo said in the voice of one humouring a child. She was observing the two of them with some interest, for Kestrel's confusion hadn't escaped her, nor the expression in Stuart's eyes as he continued to look at her. 'Now let's call a truce. Have some more coffee, Kestrel?'

'No, no, I'd better go—get on with—you know what,' Kestrel said, getting up abruptly and without meeting Stuart's eye. 'Thanks for the coffee, Theo—and the cake was delicious. Definitely a winner. When shall I call around tomorrow, to get the news?' She looked at Theo significantly, hoping to warn her not to let Stuart know of their plans.

'Oh, I should be back by lunchtime,'

Theo said. 'Call round then. If I'm not back by then, I'll come round to your house about teatime.'

'Right—I'll see you then. Cheerio. Goodbye, Mr King,' she added, and turned to look at him warily—but the strange feeling didn't come again, and his face seemed quite neutral.

'Goodbye,' was all he said.

CHAPTER 10

Outside in the rain again, Kestrel stopped to consider what to do next. Her stomach told her it was past lunchtime, but she felt restless. She didn't want to go home. Home all at once seemed far away, off the beaten track, away from the centre of activity. She wanted, now the campaign was decided upon, to be up and doing, to be furthering its cause every minute, and there was nothing she could do at home.

She glanced up the deserted village street, and suddenly thought of Laura. It might be as well to pay her a visit and find out if she really was anti-harrier, and if so, try to persuade her out of it. And of course she had to find out if she would put up a poster in the library. On this wet dark day the library was a pool of welcoming light. It was a handsome Victorian stone building with a sharply pointed roof, looking rather like a church. Its windows were very high, tall and narrow and its great door was set into an arched porchway with a stone mosaic of a Grecian female bearing the lamp of knowledge. A weathervane crowned with a black cockerel on the pointed rooftree completed the ecclesiastical air.

There were quite a few people in the library when Kestrel went in, but Laura was not one of them. Polly Hoxey, the under-librarian, who was the niece of Mrs Truman the vicar's wife, told Kestrel,

'Laura's gone home—she left about half an hour ago.'

'Oh—is she ill?' Kestrel asked.

'Oh no, it's her half day. Wednesday is her half day.'

'I thought that was Monday,' Kestrel said vaguely.

'No, Mondays she goes to Lowestoft to choose books,' Polly said earnestly. 'Wednesdays she takes her half day. Except sometimes we swap and she has Saturday and I have Wednesday.'

'Oh.' All this information slid over Kestrel's head. She was miles away. 'So if I go home, I'll catch her there?'

'I should think so. I don't suppose she'll be going out in this.'

'Thanks.'

'Kestrel wandered away again, and Polly Hoxey watched her with a half smile on her face, for Miss O'Connor had been in a minute ago to renew *A Week of Passion* and tell her that Kestrel Richards and that young man from Norwich were having coffee together in the craft shop—alone! So it was no wonder, thought Polly, that she seemed in a dream. He was, after all, a very handsome young man. She gave a short sigh, and went back to *Lord of the Rings,* which she had been reading under the desk for the past six weeks, and which looked like lasting her until Christmas.

A small wet lane between Cosser's and the dairy led to the footpath which led to Laura's bungalow. Halfway along it Kestrel was joined by Larch, who greeted her with a penetrating miaou and then bolted ahead of her, his tail upright like a standard.

When Kestrel reached the bungalow Laura was waiting for her at the back door.

'Oh, it's you,' she said. 'Larch told me someone was coming, but I couldn't think who it could be. Come in,' she added, surveying Kestrel critically. 'You're very wet. Every time I see you you seem to be soaking wet.'

'It's the rain,' Kestrel explained kindly, following Laura into her deliciously snug bungalow. Laura had resisted the fashion a few years back for replacing open fires with gas or electricity, with the result that, at a time when so many people were re-opening bricked-up chimneys at great expense, she and her cat were basking in front of roaring log fires.

'Cup of tea?' Laura offered her.

'Have you eaten yet?' Kestrel asked.

'No.'

'Then I've come to lunch.'

Laura laughed. 'Nice way to put it. All right. Sardines on toast? We'll do the toast by the fire.'

'Provided you've got a toasting fork,' Kestrel said, remembering the last time she had cooked toast by the fire at Laura's. 'I haven't got asbestos hands like you.'

'Well,' said Laura when they were settled

on the hearthrug with Larch idly cleaning himself between them, 'to what do I owe the pleasure of this visit? Or was it just for lunch?'

Kestrel considered and then, not being much of a one for tact or beating around the bush, said,

'I wanted to find out how you stand. We're starting a campaign to protect the harriers, and I wanted to know if you're pro or anti.'

'Why must I be one or the other?' Laura asked. 'Dear Kestrel, you're so very forthright, like a Roman soldier—"Who is not for us, is against us". But I can see merit on both sides. I don't think I want to be categorised.'

'All right, I don't ask you to declare on one side or the other. I just want to know if you'll help us. Or if you won't, if you'll try to stop us.'

'What in particular do you want me to do?' Laura asked, a gleam of amusement in her eyes which Kestrel didn't see.

'Well, Theo's doing some posters to advertise a meeting on Sunday in the village hall, and I wondered if you'd put one up in the library where it'll be seen. Practically everyone goes into the library—it'd be a good place to have one.'

'I'm flattered that you think the library is such a pulse-point in the village. But let me see—a poster, eh? It might be a little awkward for me, you know—being a headquarters for both sides.'

'What do you mean?' Kestrel asked suspiciously.

'Well, Stuart King does come into the library quite a lot—a couple of times a day, you know—and he mightn't find it welcoming to see your poster on the wall. Awkward for me, you see.'

Kestrel looked up, about to protest, and saw Laura's suppressed smile and realised that she was teasing. She felt rather put out for a moment, not knowing whether her request had been refused or not. Then she thought of Stuart King going into the library twice a day and asked,

'Why does he come in so often? Is he a very fast reader?'

Laura pretended to be hurt. 'That isn't very flattering,' she said. 'He comes in to see me, of course. You don't mean to say it never crossed your mind? We have a lot in common, Stuart and I.'

'Do you call him Stuart?' Kestrel tried to

135

make her voice sound neutral, but failed. Laura looked at her kindly.

'Bless you, you transparent thing,' she said. 'Is the village propaganda beginning to convince you?'

'What do you mean?' Kestrel asked defensively.

'Are you beginning to care about him? Ah, I know you'll deny it hastily and strenuously, so I'll save you the trouble, and simply reassure you that he comes into the library mainly for a chat. He's a very lonely person, and there isn't anyone with whom he can be friendly.'

'Except you,' Kestrel said in a small voice. Why did it bother her? Laura's question, to which she had not demanded an answer, rankled in Kestrel's mind. Did she begin to care? She hoped not.

'Except me. And Theo, I suppose, since he tells me he goes there too.'

'And that means that you can't support the campaign?'

'I can see merit on both sides, Kestrel,' Laura said. 'I understand what the birds mean to you and your father. And I can understand what his job means to Stuart. And putting my personal feelings for you and him aside, I understand that it is desirable to have these birds breeding here again, but on the other hand I don't think you can halt progress. You can't win this battle, you know. You've no weapons. You have no pressure to bring to bear on the developers, and there will be a lot of people to oppose you, because there are a lot of people in this village who would welcome the new houses and the new customers.'

'Shopkeepers,' Kestrel said. 'Of course, they care only about trade. But you're wrong about pressure. We're going to get a lot of publicity for this campaign, and it's going to make the developers, whoever *they* are, feel very uncomfortable. We *will* win.'

'Well, I can't say I hope you do, because I'm remaining strictly neutral,' Laura said, 'but I will put your poster up. If Theo's doing it, it will be a work of art anyway, so that will be justification enough. And I dare say I can explain it away to Stuart.'

'Oh, Stuart!' said Kestrel in disgust.

There was good news for her when she next saw her father, at teatime, for the harriers had come back, and he had seen them both near the nest. A weight seemed to lift from Kestrel's heart, for she had feared all day, without even realising it, that the campaign would come too late to help. The rain had eased to a fine mist, but the cloud cover looked settled, and the weather forecast promised more rain the next day, so there was just room for hope.

Mr Richards was interested to hear of Theo's plan for an appeal on *Roundabout*.

'That's just the right sort of programme for it, too,' he said. 'The local people all watch it, I know, and it has an intimate way of presenting its news that makes people care about it.'

'It isn't settled yet, but Theo said she was sure she could persuade the man, and I don't think she'd say that unless she were *really* sure.'

'So now we know what Theo does for a living?' Mr Richards smiled.

'I don't know that we do,' Kestrel said slowly. 'I mean, I know it's something to do with television, but exactly what she does I've no idea.'

'Ask her tomorrow,' Mr Richards suggested. 'I phoned the RSPB this afternoon, by the way.'

'Oh good! What did they say?'

'They were very interested in our campaign, and have promised to send someone down to speak on Sunday. They'll confirm by letter tomorrow who it's to be. And there *was* a reply from them to my letter here when I got back, saying that someone would be coming down tomorrow to see the birds, and hoping I'd be able to show them the place.'

'So you're getting the credit for spotting them,' Kestrel said. 'Good, I'm pleased.'

Choir-practice was at seven o'clock, and after tea Kestrel washed and changed and set off for the church. The rain had almost stopped, but remembering Theo's caustic comments about her hair she put on a headscarf, though it felt rather awkward. Perhaps it *was* time she took a little care of her appearance, she thought, and then wondered awkwardly whether the thought had anything to do with Stuart King's being in the village.

Bother Laura, she thought, why did she have to say that about me beginning to care? Now I shan't be easy with myself. She asked herself the same question, but she could give no satisfactory answer either way. The man's face was in her mind so often, but she did not know, in all honesty, what she felt about him.

She was early, but when she arrived at

the church there were already quite a few people there—those who came early for every event, and stayed late, afraid to miss anything. The church was warm and rather stuffy, for all the paraffin heaters were alight, and Miss O'Connor, who played the organ, was already seated and rocking herself to and fro in a practice run of her piece for Sunday. She was a tall woman, and very thin, so thin that the sight of her legs gave Kestrel real pain, for they looked as though the bones were about to break out through the skin. She had bright orange hair, permed very tight and cut very short, so that as she swayed back and forth on her organ stool she looked rather like a pom-pom dahlia in a high wind.

Mrs Dorrit was there, of course, for there was nothing that happened in the village that Mrs Dorrit didn't make herself a part of. She was rather a trial to the vicar, who was a musical man, for she had one of those powerful, nasal voices so often found in church choirs, and she insisted on singing the hymns very slowly and lugubriously. However much the vicar tried to liven up the beat of the hymns, the sheer weight of her voice singing half a beat behind everyone else and drawing out the last words of every line in a plaintive sob was enough to slow the entire choir. By the end of the hymn they were almost at a standstill, and even the happiest hymns sounded like dirges.

Mrs Dorrit was there now, talking to Mrs Baldergammon and Mrs Farthing and loudly criticising the flower arrangements which, that week, were the charge of Mrs Cosser, a meek unassuming woman who always dreaded her turn at the flowers for that very reason.

'She ent got no sense of colour,' Mrs Dorrit was saying, just as she had said last Sunday when Mrs Cosser's 'turn' started, thereby reducing Mrs Cosser to tears. 'All that white and yeller together, makes you feel bilious, it do really. You got to 'ave some red, stands to reason, or some blue. White and yeller, nothin' but white and yeller, it's 'orrible.'

At that moment she spotted Kestrel trying to make it to the vestry without being seen, and called her over with her booming voice.

'Ah Kestrel, there you are! Vicar's been telling us about this 'ere campaign for your birds. Fair set on it, he is, but I don't know as it's right. They're God's creatures, Mrs Dorrit, he says to me, but I says to him that may be vicar, I says, but you can't say as what we ent God's creatures too, and who's to say we shouldn't build *our* nests where we wants to, that's what I says to him.' She nodded round at her companions who looked suitably impressed. Kestrel's heart sank a little. If Mrs Dorrit declared against the campaign she could have quite an effect on the village, at least on the married women, who tended to follow her lead. Of course, there were quite a few people who would automatically be *for* anything she was against, but on the whole Kestrel thought she'd rather have Mrs Dorrit on her side.

'But don't you think we've got a duty to protect creatures smaller and weaker than ourselves?' she said, and then, thinking of something that would appeal to Mrs Dorrit, she added, 'and after all, they're our birds, Wesslingham birds, and why should they be driven out by Londoners? It's Londoners who'll be moving into these houses, you know. They aren't building houses for Wesslingham folk—just for foreigners.'

'That's right,' Mrs Dorrit nodded to Mrs Baldergammon. 'Not but what foreigners is all right in the summer—'

'We're used to them in the summer,' Mrs Baldergammon agreed. 'And what with the ice-cream and all the extra stamps for postcards and suchlike we see quite a lot of them—'

'As I was saying,' Mrs Dorrit interrupted her sternly, 'foreigners is all very well in the summer, but what do we want with them here all the year round? Who're they to tell us not to 'ave birds on our own marshes? Who do they think they are?'

Kestrel was just wondering whether to attempt a further clarification when Jim Cosser, one of the choir's best baritones, came forward from the choir stalls where he had been keeping out of the way.

'That's all very well for you, Jessie Dorrit,' he said slowly. 'You don't have your living to make. You live on your pension and what Sid left you, God rest him, so it's all one to you if they come or don't come. But me and Mary've got to make our living from the shop, and the more people there are to buy stuff off'v us, the better for us.'

He glanced across at Kestrel. 'Course, I've nothing against the birds, specially if they're as rare as what you say they

143

are, Kestrel, and I'm a great admirer of your Dad, you know that.' And then his eyes moved back, venomously, to Mrs Dorrit, whose comments on his wife's flower arrangement he could not help but have heard. 'But people ought to think twice before they try and drive customers away from honest folks' shops, especially when they live off the fat of the land themselves.'

'Who lives off the fat of the land, tell me that, Jim Cosser?' Mrs Dorrit retorted angrily. 'Who bought a new coat at Easter, with a fur collar, when other folks have to make do with what they've had for three years, *and* bought at the Jumble what Vicar held for the disaster fund, time they was flooded over to Southwick?'

'It's none of your business if I buy my wife a new coat,' Jim Cosser began hotly, when the vicar, coming in from the vestry, interrupted with a cough.

'I think we should remember that this is God's house,' he said meaningfully.

'Sorry, Vicar,' Jim Cosser said, and gave Mrs Dorrit a glare that would have melted the Gorgon, but merely slid off that lady's iron visage. Kestrel moved across to where the vicar was standing and said, softly,

'I see sides are already being taken on the issue, though I'm not sure if it's for the right reasons.'

'Yes, I know what you mean,' Mr Truman said, 'but it's bound to happen in a village. By the way, Theo's told me about your plan to go on the television with an appeal, and I must say I think it's an excellent idea! It will win over half the village, and we'll be able to get support from others in the area too. If the programme goes out tomorrow we'll be able to advertise the meeting in Southwick and Lesston and other villages in the area.'

'Good idea,' Kestrel said eagerly. 'After all, the Wessle Marsh is not only our concern, and the harrier is Suffolk's bird—the whole of Suffolk.'

'The principle involved should concern everyone in East Anglia,' said Mr Truman, soaring to the heights. 'I don't see why we shouldn't get our MP along to this meeting too. We'll really stir 'em up!'

Kestrel smiled. 'After a day of half-heartedness, it's good to find someone else who believes in this as strongly as I do.'

'I think,' began the vicar, but what he

thought was not to be disclosed, for he was distracted by the door of the church opening and admitting the other five male members of the choir in a body. 'Dear me, look at the time. I think we'd better start, you know, or choir-practice will overrun into bell-ringing, and that will never do.' He clapped his hands. 'Can we take our places, please? We'll start without the other ladies, I'm sure they'll be along in a moment.'

'I just see Mrs Mayhew, Vicar,' Mr Barrow volunteered, 'taking the baby up Jackson's. She'll be along any minute.'

'Good, good, we'll start with the collection hymn, shall we? Descant on alternate verses and the last verse,' said the vicar, raising his baton.

CHAPTER 11

Thursday dawned as drearily as Kestrel could have hoped. True, it wasn't actually raining, but the sky was dank and sodden, and lowered over a green, wet world and half-leafed trees that cowered under the imminent threat of rain. She looked out from her bedroom window over the peculiarly grey-green stretch of the marshes and noticed the morning activity of the waterfowl. Nice weather for ducks, as they say!

At breakfast her father reminded her that the man from the RSPB was coming that morning to see the harriers.

'I shall take him straight over there, and then I think bring him back here for lunch. Is there anything to eat?' Mr Richards asked.

'Not so's you'd notice,' Kestrel said cheerfully through a mouthful of toast. It was typical of her father, she thought, to decide to bring someone to lunch and worry about food afterwards. 'But I can go to the shops this morning if you like. The house could do with a bit of a spruce too, if we're having visitors.'

'Yes, I suppose it could be tidier,' her father said vaguely, looking round at the heaps of clean clothes that were lying everywhere since Kestrel had done the washing. Just as washing had to wait until one or other of them felt driven to do it, so did the ironing.

'We could have a quick blast at it

now,' Kestrel suggested. 'If I put these clothes somewhere, you could get out the Hoover and do the carpets while I dust.'

They looked at each other across the table for a moment in a kind of despair at the mere thought of it, and then they sighed in unison.

'I suppose it must be done,' her father said. 'I must say, when I remember how spotless the house used to look when your mother was alive, I am consumed with admiration for her. She never actually seemed to be doing anything, what's more. I suppose that's the definition of an artist—a person who makes a difficult task seem easy.'

'Come on, Dad, I know you. You're hoping to tempt me into a discussion to put off the evil hour,' Kestrel smiled, and her father smiled back at her. 'How ever did you guess?' he said.

In fifteen minutes the house was what Kestrel called 'bachelor clean', which is to say clean enough to pass muster as long as no-one inspected too closely, and she and her father came together again at the dining table to discuss the food. Though an indifferent, not to say inert, housekeeper, Mr Richards was an excellent cook when he troubled, mainly because he disliked badly-cooked food and there had been, in Kestrel's childhood, no-one but him to cook it.

'There isn't much doing in the garden at the moment,' he said thoughtfully, 'but we still have plenty of last year's onions and some carrots in store.'

'Some kind of stew or casserole, then,' Kestrel suggested. 'You could put it on before you went out and it could keep cooking on a low light until you were ready for it.'

'Yes, good idea. Perhaps a veal ragoût, then? There's half a pint of sour cream in the fridge I can use to cheer it up.'

'Is there?' Kestrel said, puzzled. 'I don't remember buying sour cream.'

'You didn't,' he replied. 'It was fresh cream to have with fruit, but I forgot about it. Mrs Pendle from the farm gave it to me as I was passing last week.'

'Oh. Well, in that case, what are you going to give the man for dessert?'

Mr Richards thought for a moment, and then his brow cleared. 'The only thing we have plenty of is eggs, so we'll have a sweet omelette. So all we need to buy is veal and some mushrooms. Shall I go down, or will you?'

'You go, then you can take the bike,' Kestrel said, remembering the crash at Dodman's Corner. She didn't want to tempt fate again. 'I'll start chopping vegetables.'

By the time the man from the RSPB, most appropriately named Mr Nightingale, arrived, the ragoût was simmering slowly in the oven of the kitchen range, and no-one would have guessed the state the house had been in at breakfast time. Mr Nightingale was small and balding and bespectacled, and for some reason this was just the way Kestrel had expected the man from the RSPB to look. This realisation made her uneasy, for she didn't like to categorise people, and the thought that there might be a 'type' in her imagination for a bird-lover shamed her. Had she not thought the worse of Stuart King for referring to bird freaks, or whatever his expression had been? And yet she was falling into the same trap, she who had a father who was nothing like the public's image of an ornithologist.

After some preliminary chat and a cup of coffee, Mr Richards said,

'Well, old chap, are you ready to go? I hope you brought some gumboots—it's pretty wet across the marshes.'

'Oh yes, they're in my car—I'll go and fetch them. You've been having a lot of rain just recently, I understand.'

'Yes, and fortunately, as it's turned out,' Mr Richards said. 'Are you coming with us, Kestrel?'

'Oh—er—no, I don't think I will,' Kestrel said, for she felt she would rather not spend the morning with Mr Nightingale after having just typecast him in her mind. 'I think I'll go down to the village and do some canvassing—that's the way I can be of most use, I think.'

'As you wish,' he replied. 'I don't know what time we'll be back for lunch, but if we come in before you I'll leave you some in the cool oven.'

'Thanks, Dad. I'll see you later then.'

It was actually raining now, steadily from a dark grey sky, but Kestrel had grown so used to the wet that, like a bargee, she scarcely noticed it. She passed Mr Nightingale's red Escort, the only spot of bright colour in view, and walked down the lane to Dodman's. There she paused for a moment, wondering whether to stop

151

by and canvass Mr Ambrose, and decided against it. It was a waste of time, really, for he would come to the meeting anyway, since he went to every free entertainment within range, whether or not he thought he'd enjoy it. Also, she felt pretty sure he'd vote for her when the time came, having known her from childhood and being fond of her. So she passed his cottage by and went on towards the village.

Might as well start with a hard case, she thought, and stopped at the first house she passed, which was the end one of a row of Edwardian terraced houses of the type known as 'artisans' cottages'. It was called Myrtle Cottage, its name appearing in stone over the door, but it was more generally known as Jackson's, for it was the Jacksons who lived there.

Mr Jackson was out of work. He had been born out of work, and intended to die that way, but as a face-saver he had always to pretend that it was the state of the country that caused him to live off the dole and spend his days reading the racing-page of the daily newspaper and waiting for the Bell to open.

Partly out of laziness and partly to improve his income from the government,

Jackson had given Mrs Jackson seven children, which ensured she stayed home too, so there was always someone in whatever the time of day. Despite her continual state of harassment Mrs Jackson was a good-natured, friendly soul, who liked nothing better than to have someone drop in and give her an excuse to stop whatever she was doing and make tea. It might have been her sociable nature that decided her to become the village childminder, or it might simply have seemed the natural thing to do, on the basis that she had so many a few more would make no difference.

Whatever the reason, the fact remained that if anyone in the village wanted a child minded for whatever reason, there was no question of ringing round for a babysitter—it was 'I'm taking Baby up Jackson's', and Baby would be kept until called for, in exchange for a pound of marge or a dozen eggs or money if there was any around, which there usually wasn't.

So Kestrel, as she walked up the path to the battered front door, knew that someone would be in and that she would be asked in for a cup of tea and listened to, but she also knew that Mr Jackson would be agin it, on the grounds that stopping the building would put men out of work. She mentally girded her loins, and knocked.

By lunchtime, she had learnt one thing about canvassing, and that was that the canvasser needed an endless capacity for tea. At every house where her knock was answered she had to accept a cup, and by the time she reached Pendle's Farm at the other end of the village she was awash, and glad to accept a piece of cake, despite the warning that it was 'a bit on the stale side', in the hope that it might soak up some of the liquid.

The canvassing had gone well, though, mainly because it was the women she had been speaking to, most of the menfolk being out at work. She guessed that the men would tend to look on the practical side, and dismiss ecological arguments as airy-fairy nothings.

She had intended to work her way down one side of the street and up the other, but she was now at the far end of the village and very hungry, so she decided to make her way straight home for lunch, stopping only at the craft shop to see if Theo was back with the news about the television programme. Canvassing took longer than she had realised.

Theo was back. She was sitting at her desk in the window of the shop working on a poster, and she waved cheerfully to Kestrel as soon as she saw her, so Kestrel guessed it was good news.

'Everything's okay,' Theo said as Kestrel came in, 'it's all laid on for tomorrow, and Tony thinks it's just the thing for local interest.'

'Oh, terrific!' Kestrel said. 'So what happens? Do they come out here or do we go in to them?'

'Both,' Theo said. 'They want to have a bit of film of the birds themselves and then to follow that with a studio interview with you—'

'Me?' Kestrel said in surprise. 'Why not you?'

'Because they're your birds, numbskull,' Theo said.

'They're my father's if they're anyone's. Or the vicar's. Why not one of them?'

'A young girl, especially a pretty one, has more appeal than a middle-aged man, however illustrious.'

'But—'

'Look, you want to get support for the campaign, don't you? Then stop griping.'

'It's just that I've never been on television before. I wouldn't know what to do.'

'Believe me,' Theo said patiently, 'they'll know. They're quite experienced, in fact. And if they'd wanted Elizabeth Taylor they'd have asked for her.'

'All right,' Kestrel said, making a face. 'I get the general idea. What actually happens, anyway?'

'Well, they'll be sending down a team with a hand camera tomorrow morning, and you'll have to take them to see the birds. They're coming early, as I said it was the best time to see the birds, and also to leave as much time as possible in case they don't appear. You have to be patient when you're filming animals.'

'Supposing they don't appear at all?' Kestrel asked in a small voice.

'Oh, in that case they'll just have to use photographs, and some film of the area, but it won't be so effective as some film of the birds live, on the spot. However, we shall see. They might do a short interview with your father, since he is quite famous and he is really the discoverer of the birds—' she shut Kestrel up with a glance as the latter was about to add something about the vicar.

'And then,' Theo went on firmly, 'you'll have to go in to the studio in Norwich in the afternoon and record an interview to go on after the outdoor film. They may want to have you talking over the film, depending on whether or not they get anything that needs explaining—like the birds feeding or building a nest or something.'

'It won't go out live, then?' Kestrel asked, not knowing whether she was glad or sorry.

'No, so you should be able to get back in time to see yourself. They want you down at the studio for two-thirty. They'll pay your fare, of course.'

'Of course?' Kestrel didn't think it was as obvious as all that.

'Certainly. Go up by train, and get a taxi from the station. And there'll be a fee as well, but I should think it'll only be standard.'

'I have to pay them?' Kestrel asked, startled. Theo burst out laughing.

'Oh really, Kestrel! They pay you, of

course, but as I said it won't be much. Now, is there anything you want to ask?'

'Won't you be there?'

'Oh no, I'll be keeping up the good work at this end.'

'I see. But what shall I say? Will I have a script to learn?'

'You'll just sit at a desk with the interviewer—I don't know who that will be, but you've seen all the *Roundabout* team on the box a dozen times so they won't seem strange to you. You'll sit at a desk, and the interviewer will ask you questions, and you'll just answer them. You don't have to worry about what to say; that's the interviewer's job, to keep you talking. You'll enjoy it, don't worry.'

'And what should I wear?'

'Anything you like, but I think it ought to be neat and tidy. And do something with your hair—there's nothing worse on television than a person who continually pushes their hair back from their face.'

'All right, I'll do it up. Anything else?'

'Nothing I can think of. But don't worry, you'll enjoy it. It'll be a new experience for you. Now then, you'd better see about distributing the posters I've finished. I've only done three so far, but I'll do some more today and put them up tomorrow. What do you think of them?'

They really were impressive, and Kestrel told her so with enthusiasm. Each carried a picture of a harrier flying against a pale blue background. 'That's the sky, in case you don't recognise it,' Theo said solemnly. The wording was in a deep crimson, which stood out really well against the pale blue.

'Eyecatching,' Kestrel said, standing back to get the effect across the room. 'I'll get them up straight away—one for the post office, one for the Dog and Duck, and one for the library, I think. They're the most important sites. And then,' she remembered, 'I'll have some lunch.'

Mr Baldergammon made no problem about putting up the poster, and said that they would both be along to the meeting after evensong. Kestrel told them about the television programme, and they were quite excited, promised to watch it and to tell everyone else about it too.

159

'You should have put something about it on the poster—you know, like what they do in the Co-op window—'As seen on television'.' He laughed heartily at his own joke, and Kestrel smiled politely.

'That Mrs Dorrit will be green with envy,' Mrs Baldergammon said confidentially. 'She's always been on about her niece what was in the pantomime up Lowestoft, but *she* never got on the telly, even though she did go to stage school. Wait till I tell her.'

Kestrel gave up trying to sort out the she's and her's, said goodbye, and headed back through the village towards the library. It was still raining in a half-hearted way, and as she passed the Bell she wondered what Stuart King was doing with himself. She supposed there must be something for him to do about the site even when it rained, and therefore she was surprised when she reached the door of the library to see him inside. Of course, it might be his lunch hour, but he looked very comfortable and very much a permanent fixture, for he was sitting on a high stool on the far side of Laura's Dickensian desk, and he was talking to Laura and laughing, perhaps telling her a joke, while she worked.

As Kestrel watched, standing looking through the glass door at the lit-up scene inside, like the little match girl, she saw Laura glance up at Stuart and smile at something he had said, and there was something very cosy about the pair of them. His head seemed very close to Laura's dark curly one, and their smiles for each other seemed very warm and intimate, as if they were old friends—at least.

She had forgotten for a moment what she was doing there, and had forgotten also that she could be seen as well as see. Stuart glanced up, his attention perhaps attracted by her shadow at the door, and for a moment he looked at her in surprise. Laura looked up at him, and then towards the door, and Kestrel, in some confusion backed away, stared back at the pair of them for a moment, and then turned and ran back through the rain towards home.

What would they think of her, spying on them like that, was the thought in the top of her mind. But underneath were darker thoughts, and she did not care to analyse them.

CHAPTER 12

And why not? she thought over and over again as she ate her veal ragoût and rice in solitary splendour. Her father and Mr Nightingale had evidently eaten and departed their separate ways: there were dirty dishes in the sink and the red Escort had gone from their lane.

Why not? Why shouldn't he like Laura. Why should she be jealous? She had never given him anything but abuse and hostility, so it was utterly unreasonable to expect him to feel anything towards her, except possibly wariness. Laura was a lovely person, marvellous company, very witty and amusing. What had she, Kestrel, to go on but that one moment when she imagined he looked at her strangely? That and the fact that for years she had occupied the position of Miss Wesslingham (some honour!) and had got used to being considered attractive.

Well, pride went before a fall true enough, and quite rightly too. She could do with taking down a peg. Kestrel scraped her plate clean and then realised guiltily that she hadn't tasted a mouthful of it, though it had looked and smelled delicious. She thought of her father labouring over it, and in her present overwrought state that was enough to make her burst into tears. She had a lovely cry for ten minutes or so, and felt better immediately.

Reason prevailing, she told herself that her father wouldn't care twopence whether she had tasted his veal whatnot or fed it to the cat, and that since she didn't care twopence for Mr Stuart King in all his glory, why should she feel piqued that he preferred Laura's company to hers? All she had needed was an excuse for a bit of a weep to let off steam—for she had been wound up tight as a drum all week over the fate of the harriers—and now she had had it, she could relax.

She contemplated finishing her meal as the others had with a sweet omelette, which she adored, but simply couldn't be bothered to go to the trouble of making one just for herself. So she cut a doorstep of bread, buttered it, loaded it with gooseberry jam (Laura's home-made, as it happened) and went to sit on the window-seat in her father's room to eat it, with Bewick's Book of Birds open on her knee. She was quite happy again.

The rain stopped around teatime, and when her father had settled down with a book, Kestrel decided to go down to the Dog and Duck and see if she could persuade someone to play darts or bar billiards with her. It was a pleasant evening, cooler, with a break in the clouds, but with a touch of colour streaking the horizon. Red sky at night, sailor's delight, she told herself. I'm in the unenviable position of having to want bad weather. But just for tonight it can do no harm if it stays dry.

The Dog and Duck was quite crowded, Thursday night being pay night for both the town workers and the farm labourers, and there was no chance of getting on the bar billiards table, but she put her name down to chalk on the dart board, and while she was still waiting Tim O'Connor came in and walked straight over to her as if he had expected her to be there.

'Hello, Kess,' he said. She frowned, having always disliked the abbreviation. 'Got your name down? Good, then I'll partner you.'

'It's singles,' she pointed out, glad of the excuse.

'Won't be for long,' he said, and raised his voice to call to the two people playing at that moment. 'Here, Bill, Stan! How about doubling up? Else some of us will never get a game—look, there's six waiting now.'

'I don't mind,' said Stan amiably, 'but then I'm losin'. What about you, Bill?'

So it was decided, and she found herself bound to spend the evening in Tim's company. Not what she would have chosen, but as it turned out the evening went quite pleasantly, for when they got on the board, they won, and won the next game, and the next. It's pleasant to win at any time, and since the rule in darts is that if you win you stay on to play the next challengers, it meant that she could play all evening.

It is no longer very surprising to find girls playing darts, and playing well, but it was sufficiently unusual in Wesslingham for Kestrel to find herself the centre of attention, which was very bad for her character, of course, but very nice for her ego. A small crowd gathered round the dartboard, cheering on Kestrel and her partner, and the older men in the crowd were teasing her and paying her outrageous compliments, while Tim basked in reflected glory and had more pints bought for him than since his birthday.

Having just won another game in fine style, Kestrel turned from collecting her darts from the board amid loud cheers and saw Stuart King standing half in and half out of the door, looking at her with a quizzical smile. The grin slid off Kestrel's face, and as her eyes met his for a moment across the crowded bar she felt the same odd feeling of kinship that she had felt that time in Theo's shop. She had the feeling that he had come there to find her, and that he would come across and say—she didn't know what, but something important. His smile broadened, and an answering smile began to curve her lips.

And at that moment Tim pushed his way to her, blocking her view of Stuart, and flinging an arm round her neck he gave her a noisy kiss on the cheek. Kestrel jerked her head away and pulled back angrily, and there were catcalls and cries of 'Look out, Tim!' and 'You'll get your face slapped!' Tim smirked in a silly way and pretended to duck, and Kestrel pushed past him with a contemptuous glare. But the doorway was empty. The door of the pub swung gently; Stuart was gone.

Friday dawned almost spring-like, a watery blue sky showing patchily through clouds, and a thin sunlight broken up by showers. A fitful kind of day, Kestrel thought as she dressed, but probably better than steady rain as far as the filming went. Her worry was that the weather would be good enough to permit building to start again, and that the birds would therefore not appear.

She and her father breakfasted on porridge and toast, and they were just finishing when the camera crew arrived in a rather battered Land Rover. Kestrel jumped up and ran out to meet them—two duffle-coated young men and a straggly-haired girl in an anorak. They were not in the least glamorous, and though a little disappointed, Kestrel was relieved too that they seemed easy and approachable.

'I hope you've brought wellingtons with you,' she called as they got out of the car. 'It's terribly wet.'

'So we were warned,' the girl said. 'I'm afraid I don't possess a pair, but I'm wearing stout shoes.'

She lifted her foot to show Kestrel, who shook her head doubtfully.

'The mud will come over the top. What size feet have you? Perhaps I can lend you a pair.'

'I told you so, Doreen,' said one of the men, while the other opened the back of the Land Rover to get out his own boots and the equipment.

'Size five,' the girl said. 'By the way, I'm Doreen Good, assistant producer, and these are Nick and Terry, camera and sound.'

They nodded hello, and Mr Richards came out to be introduced as well.

'I think we should go straight away to see the birds,' he said, 'in case the building work starts again and they're frightened off.'

'Right-oh,' said Terry. 'You lead on.'

'I think, since your equipment looks rather heavy, we'd better drive through the village and get to the nest across the building site. Otherwise you might all sink without trace under the weight of your cameras.'

This sensible suggestion was acted upon, and they all piled into the Land Rover. While Kestrel directed the driver, Doreen sat in the back with Mr Richards taking down notes while he told her the history of the birds and the battle.

It was nearly eight o'clock by the time they reached the building site, and already there were men there, wandering about and smoking in an apparently aimless way, which would have told anyone who thought about it that their day didn't officially start until eight. Kestrel crossed her fingers, and under their slightly surprised stare the five of them picked their way over the mud towards the marshes. Doreen now safe in a pair of Kestrel's boots that were too small for her.

They made their way to the hide, the two men carrying the camera between them. Though it was called a hand camera, it was quite big, and was designed to be held with the bulk of it resting on the shoulder, 'like a bazooka', Nick explained, and Kestrel nodded wisely, not knowing what a bazooka was when it was at home. They were very quick and quiet at their preparations, and when Mr Richards had pointed out to them the location of the nest, and they had let him and Kestrel have a look through the camera to see how the zoom worked, they all became very still and waited hopefully for the birds to appear.

If only the men on the site haven't scared them off, Kestrel thought. She had binoculars with her, as did her father, and from time to time she swung them from the nest onto the building site, trying to see what the men were doing. There seemed to be some digging, and others were marking out squares with pegs and string, but so far no machines had been started up, and as the morning broadened she began to hope that they would not be used today.

At one time Stuart appeared in the lenses of her binoculars, and she moved them away quickly fearing he would see her, before she realised what a silly thing to do that was. And then she saw the harriers. She stiffened and then looked round quickly to see if the others had spotted them. Her father was just pointing them out to Nick the cameraman, and he was making the okay sign with his finger and thumb. Terry was getting ready with his sound equipment, in case the birds should come close enough for him to record their cry.

It was as if the birds had known they were to be on television. They flew in together, going first to the nest, and then making a few runs up and down the edge of the building site in a kind of aerial reconnaissance. They flew back and forth from one perching-place to another, calling to each other in their clear, loud voices, and then they began their mating dance.

The five watchers in the hide were held spellbound as the harriers put on a full show, doing everything in their repertoire as if they knew their fate depended on it. After the first minute Kestrel became unaware of the sound of the camera beside her, or of the other people watching with her. It was magical. Climbing, banking, spinning like falling leaves, stooping, somersaulting, the dance of the air went on, with such wild, free grace in the performers that it made Kestrel's throat ache with the beauty of it.

How could anyone, having seen that, not take the birds to their heart? It was something beyond price, something that could not be measured against mere worldly gain, against bricks and mortar, or money, or jobs. The birds played with the air in a wild exuberance, and the watchers could not take their eyes off them.

When at last the dance ended and the

birds flew away, low over the marshes, and the camera had followed them out of sight, there was a silence until at last Doreen sighed.

'Lovely,' she said.

'Fantastic film,' Nick said enthusiastically. 'I hadn't hoped for anything like this. Tony will be delighted—he was all set to use stills if necessary, but this will be a winner. Did you get anything?' he asked Terry.

'I'm not sure until I hear it over. There was a lot of wind. It may block out the calls.'

While they were talking, Kestrel was looking across at the building site through the binoculars, for she felt sure that the men over there must all have been watching; and she was astonished to see them looking only at the mud under their feet and the tools in their hands, oblivious of the fact that an aerial ballet had just been performed, free, for anyone who would only lift up his head. Stuart was nowhere to be seen, and she was sorry. She had hoped that he too might see, and be converted.

'I'm very pleased that the birds came so close,' Mr Richards said. 'The fact that they are still doing their mating display shows that they haven't been too badly upset, so there is still hope. The men aren't using any machines today, of course, which makes a difference.' He looked at the television people. 'What would you like to do? Do you want to wait here, or try following them up? I think I know where they will be.'

'Oh, I think we've got enough film,' Doreen said, 'haven't we, Nick?'

'Plenty,' Nick said. 'I'll hardly have to edit it at all. The shame of it is we probably won't be able to show half of it, unless Tony stretches the item and cuts down on something else. Still, it can always be shown again.'

'All we want now, I think,' Doreen went on, 'is some wide-angle shots of the marsh in general, a sweep taking in your house, and perhaps a shot of the church—it looks rather grand and lonely there. And a couple of feet of the nest in relation to the building site, so the audience can see the problem. How are we for sound out here, Terry?'

The man, squatting over his equipment, shook his head. 'Too much wind. I'd rather do it indoors.'

'Okay,' Doreen said. 'So what we'll do is this—we'll take some shots of the marsh, and then we'll go back to the house and record, sound only, me asking you a few questions in case they want something to go over the film—okay?'

'Certainly,' said Mr Richards. 'Whatever you like.'

'I'd better run on home and tidy up, then,' Kestrel said, smiling. 'Dad, you can take care of them, can't you, while I go on home? I'll take the short cut over the marsh, and get some coffee on.'

'What a marvellous idea,' said Doreen. 'I don't know about you, but I'm freezing.'

'It's all the standing still that does it,' Kestrel said, and took her departure.

The others were not long behind her, though she did manage to have coffee and sandwiches ready for them, for which they were grateful. Afterwards they recorded a short interview with Mr Richards in the dining-room, and then packed up and took their leave.

'I shall be seeing you again this afternoon,' of course,' said Doreen as she shook hands with Kestrel. 'At the studio.'

'So you will,' Kestrel said, thinking with some excitement about the afternoon.

'But probably only to wave to,' Doreen

went on. 'I don't actually interview you or anything.'

And Kestrel noticed that there was a tinge of envy in her voice, as if to interview Kestrel was something to be desired. It just showed, she thought afterwards, that however glamorous someone else's life seems, there's always something more that *they* want.

On which piece of philosophy, she went upstairs to choose something to wear.

CHAPTER 13

It was quite a treat for Kestrel to take the pay-train in to Norwich. Of course while she had been working she had taken the train in to Lowestoft each day, but that was such a short journey it had been rather like taking a bus—hardly worth sitting down. The journey to Norwich was quite long, for the little train chugged slowly through the countryside, stopping at every railway halt, and there was plenty of time to enjoy the scenery and look out for birds.

There were plenty of them to be seen,

for in places the railway line passed through quite wild parts, and she stored up the memory of a blue heron standing contemplating on one leg and a flight of Canada geese to tell her father about when she got home.

At Norwich she descended from the train in a leisurely manner and walked at her own pace out of the station, with the result that she was last in the queue for the taxis. It proved to her how much out of tune with town life she was, and how quickly her experience of working in Lowestoft had slid off her. Stuart King no doubt would have jumped off the train before it stopped moving and pounded down the platform with his hand out ready. And then she thought, bother, I'm thinking about him again, and for the rest of her wait she forced herself to think of other things.

When at last her turn came, she felt smart enough to get into the back, instead of going in front with the driver as she had on other occasions—fairly rare—when she had taken a taxi. She had on one of her town dresses—a smart navy with white piping—and has wrestled her hair up into a kind of French pleat with drooping

176

folds at the front and over her ears. The folds didn't feel too secure, and she told herself to remember not to move her head quickly, or they would undoubtedly descend gracelessly during the crucial part of the day.

The taxi drew up outside the studios, and Kestrel was rather disappointed that the driver was not more impressed by her destination. She had expected him at least to ask her if she was 'on the telly', but he merely said good afternoon and drove away. The building itself was not impressive, being rather drab and grimy, and with nothing outside to show for itself except a small sign over the door, not even illuminated. However, a commissionaire stood just inside in full uniform with his hands behind his back, and he stepped forward attentively enough as Kestrel came in.

'—help you Miss?' he said.

'Oh, yes—I'm on *Roundabout,*' Kestrel said. The man walked over to his desk and consulted a page on a clip-board.

'Your name, Miss?'

'Richards,' she said, wondering what she would do if he said he had no record of her name. But he nodded, marked his list, and said he would call them. He dialled on the internal phone and announced her, and in a moment a girl came through some swing doors and said, smiling pleasantly,

'Miss Richards? Will you come this way, please?'

Kestrel followed the girl through the swing doors, and along a passage lined with closed doors, some of them bearing code figures, through some more swing doors, round a corner, and at last into a large room, brightly lit, that she realised was the studio. The row of desks with the diamond-patterned wall behind that she recognised from *Roundabout* was on one side of the room, and at one end of it a kind of screen with the *Roundabout* motif on it in full colour—Kestrel had only ever seen the programme in black and white.

The rest of the room was occupied with cameras, cables and chairs. A whole clutch of cables ran right across the room, and where they passed a door on the other side from where Kestrel stood they ran under a kind of wooden ramp. Using her wits, Kestrel decided this was so that the heavy cameras could be wheeled over the cables without damaging them.

She had not time to notice more,

however, for a tall and incredibly thin man, whose cheesecloth shirt seemed to cling to bare bones, came up to shake her hand and say,

'Hello! Nice of you to come. I'm Tony Flaxman, and I'm the editor of the show. Come on over and meet Bill Anderson—he's the lucky chap who'll actually be interviewing you.'

With a kind of professional ease, Tony Flaxman kept hold of her hand and led her by it across the studio towards the *Roundabout* desks where the famous man was already seated. Kestrel felt somewhat bashful, firstly because she hadn't been led anywhere by the hand since she was very small, and secondly because she knew Bill Anderson so well from the television, but of course knew him not at all in person. It was the oddest sensation, for the feeling of knowing him was so strong she half thought he would recognise her, and knowing that he wouldn't gave her the feeling of being a peeping tom. She had never met anyone famous before, and she wondered if it affected everyone that way.

There was no opportunity to ask, though. Bill Anderson stood up, stretched his hand out to her across the desk, and said,

'How do you do? I'm Bill Anderson, but please just call me Bill—everyone does.'

Kestrel took his hand shyly, and found that he was smiling a quite ravishing smile at her and looking very earnestly into her face. Automatically she smiled back at him, and when he kept hold of her hand and looked into her face just a little longer than was necessary, she realised that he was memorising her, and that it was part of his job. It made her feel at ease, for she now realised that she was to Bill Anderson much as a patient is to a doctor or dentist—merely a body with which he was to perform his task with professional skill.

'Would you just like to sit down next to Bill, Kestrel—you don't mind if I call you Kestrel, do you?—so that we can see how you are for lighting.' This from Tony Flaxman, and though Kestrel didn't care for people who asked you if you minded being called by your first name and didn't give you time to answer, she knew that this was all just a formula, and that there was no room here for personal feelings. A lot obviously had to be got through, and the best thing she could do was to go where she was pushed and say as little as possible.

In a moment she found herself sitting behind that famous desk, next to that famous man, and staring out at a rank of cameras, pointing at her like cannon, and making her feel rather special.

'Just look at me for a minute, would you?' said Bill Anderson, and she turned towards him, and found that he was looking at her and smiling that peculiarly intimate smile which, though she knew it was only professionalism, still made her smile back. 'Where did you get such an unusual Christian name?' he asked. Kestrel was startled for a moment, wondering what he was up to, and then realised that he wanted her to speak for technical reasons. So she told him. When she stopped speaking he looked towards the cameras and said,

'I think you'll have to tone down.'

Someone out beyond the cameras replied incomprehensibly, and for a while Bill Anderson and Tony Flaxman and the technician threw technical comments and questions back and forth, and now and then requested Kestrel to turn her head one way or another, or move her chair nearer or farther from the desk. Then

181

they seemed to forget her, and Tony Flaxman came over with his clip-board and talked in a low voice to Bill Anderson. Kestrel looked around her, taking the opportunity to study the studio from this new angle. What surprised her most was the number of monitor screens there were, three directly in front of the desk, and one at each end, plus three more high up near the ceiling. There were lots of people walking about purposefully, and strangest of all, a man in the costume of a Spanish dancer lounging against a table right at the back and looking very bored.

At last the two men finished their conversation, and Tony Flaxman turned to Kestrel and said,

'Sorry about that! Now Jill will take you through to make-up, and then we'll have a run through with you, and then we'll do the actual shot. The film of the birds has come out very well, by the way, and we're using a good bit of it. Wonderful actors, those birds.'

Kestrel smiled dutifully as she felt she was expected to, and got up to follow the same young girl out through the swing-doors she had noticed earlier into another corridor. As she hurried along behind the girl, feeling rather like Alice with the White Rabbit, they passed the other compère of *Roundabout*, Graham Cook. Kestrel prepared to smile at him, but he gave the merest, coldest glance and brushed past them.

Kestrel felt at once that she didn't like him as much as Bill Anderson, and then told herself not to be silly, that had she met him behind the desk and Bill Anderson in the corridor, their reactions would have been reversed. After all, why should he feel the slightest interest in a stranger being led along the corridor, as, probably, hundreds of strangers were led every day? It was only this odd business of recognising the man from the television that led her to expect anything else. She pondered on the phenomenon all the way home.

Now, however, she found herself being ushered into a tiny room with 'Make-up 3' on the door. A girl in a nylon overall was standing before the mirror which took up all the short length of the wall. Before the mirror was a low work surface cluttered with jars and bottles and pan-sticks, boxes of tissues, cotton wool, and a number of used tissues crumpled up. Before the work surface was a single chair, and in this Kestrel sat herself, meeting the make-up girl's eyes in the mirror as one does a hairdresser's.

'Hello,' she said briskly. 'Now, is there anything you want in particular? Have you brought any of your own stuff with you?'

'No,' said Kestrel, surprised. 'I hardly ever wear make-up. Was I supposed to?'

'It's just as you like. If you don't usually wear anything, I shouldn't bother. I don't think we need to do anything to you—you've got a good colour.' She placed a hand on Kestrel's head and turned it this way and that, watching the reflection critically.

'But don't I have to have special make-up for the cameras?' Kestrel asked, rather disappointed. The girl looked bored, as if she'd had the same question asked twenty times a day for the past year.

'Oh no, not nowadays. Just your ordinary make-up—for those who use it, I mean. Some people need a bit of touching up here and there, but young people don't usually need anything. Shall I put a couple of pins in your hair for you? It seems to be falling down at the back.'

'Thank you,' said Kestrel dully. Nothing

was turning out the way she'd expected.

Having pinned up her hair, the make-up girl went out, leaving Kestrel alone, and there she was left for what seemed like half an hour, though on reflection she realised it could not have been more than ten minutes. She was getting distinctly bored, when the girl Jill appeared in the doorway and said breathlessly,

'Can you come back, please? We're waiting to do your run-through.'

Kestrel fell in behind again and they scuttled back to the studio, Kestrel feeling as though she'd done something wrong, though how anyone could have expected her to know she was wanted she didn't know. In the studio she was taken again by Tony Flaxman and sat down in a seat at one end of the desk, and after a moment Bill Anderson came up and sat down beside her, giving her his famous smile and saying,

'Marvellous! You look marvellous. Okay, Tony?' he called towards the cameras, and then he turned back to Kestrel. 'Now you'll be on camera two—that's that one there. When the light goes on, that means it's working, and you'll see yourself on the monitor. But don't look at the monitor, please—you'll have plenty of time to see yourself afterwards. Right, now in a minute we'll start. When the light on the camera goes on, look at me, and just answer my questions in your normal voice. All right?'

Kestrel nodded. He smiled again. 'Don't be nervous,' he said, and she said, rather more sharply than she had meant to, 'I'm not!' He smiled bravely, 'Marvellous,' he said. She felt that he didn't really like her.

When the light on the camera went on and she looked round at him, however, his smile had all its intimate freshness, and she smiled back as before. His voice took on the tones she remembered from watching the programme at home, and she had just time to marvel that it was her he was talking to. He asked her about her father, about her helping him, about the birds and about the threat to them, and she answered quite naturally, for the way he put the questions made it seem as though he really wanted to know.

After a while someone called okay and Bill Anderson stopped abruptly and looked towards the cameras. 'How was it?' he asked.

'Okay for me,' someone replied, and someone else said rather acidly,

'Can she keep her hands still?'

Bill Anderson turned to Kestrel and translated. 'Can you keep your hands still on the desk—or keep them in your lap if you like—but don't fidget them.'

Kestrel nodded, feeling like a small child caught out in class doing something rather horrid, and Bill Anderson called back to the hidden man 'How was it for sound otherwise?' He received a reply which Kestrel couldn't hear, and then said, 'Well, why don't we go straight on with it? Can we do it now? Well, we can do that afterwards—let's get this one out of the way.'

It was all rather horrid, sitting there and being a mere useless body. If this is television, I don't want anything to do with it, Kestrel thought. However, in a moment she was told that they were going to do the real thing, and just to do what she had done before, and in a moment she saw the light go on over the camera, and out of the corner of her eye saw a picture come up on the monitor, which with great willpower she managed not to look at, and then Bill Anderson was smiling at her and asking her the exact same question as he had before.

It was that which put her off. He put the question in such an interested way, as if he really wanted to know—but she had told him the answer only minutes before. She felt she ought to vary the words she used, and yet she couldn't think of a different way of putting it. The result was that she felt stilted, and tried to cut her answers short, as if she were afraid of boring him. It was a miserable few minutes for her, and she was entirely glad when he turned from her to face the camera again, and she saw the light go off.

Tony Flaxman came over to Bill Anderson, and after a few moments' private talk, the former nodded to Kestrel and said,

'Okay, that's fine. We have all we need now. Would you like to come over here?'

She came out from behind the desk, half expecting to be told she was a miserable failure and that they wouldn't be showing the film after all. But he merely took her to one side and presented her with a biro, saying,

'That was super, thanks a lot, Kestrel. Now, if you'd just like to sign—'

'Was it really all right? I felt terribly stilted and stiff,' Kestrel interrupted him, trying to break through his professionalism.

'No, it was super, really,' he said hurriedly. 'Now if you'd just like to sign the contract—it's absolutely standard, so you don't need to read it unless you want—and the fee will be sent to you in a few days. It's just the standard fee—ten pounds.'

'All this and money too,' Kestrel joked.

'Super,' he said, and she could see he wasn't really listening, but just eager to get on with it, so she took the pen and signed where he pointed.

'What do I do now?' she asked. He looked slightly surprised.

'Oh—well—you can stay on, if you like, and watch the rest of the show. Your interview will be run through in a minute, and you can see it in one of the viewing rooms if you like.'

'You mean I'm free to go?'

'Oh yes, by all means. But do stay and watch if you'd like, and he smiled a harassed smile, remembering that she was Theo's friend. Kestrel knew she was simply being a problem, and decided to remove herself from his hair forthwith.

189

'I think I'll go and look at the shops,' she said. 'Thanks very much. I'll give Theo your love.'

'Oh yes, Theo—' he said vaguely, and by the time she had moved a step away from him he had already forgotten her existence.

She found her way out and passed by the same commissionaire.

'All right?' he said.

'Yes thank you,' she replied, and thought how his question and her answer meant equally as little. They were no more than bird calls, each acknowledging the presence of the other.

CHAPTER 14

Kestrel was glad to be finished with the television business, and with no particular thought in her head other than getting away from the place she walked through the town and found herself in the main street near the market. There was a pleasant afternoon bustle about the place which was so different from Wesslingham, where the bustle was only ever very temporary and local—around the post office on pension day, or outside the church after a Sunday service, for example.

It was good to be in town with no necessity for doing anything in particular, and she idled along the pavements, annoying faster-moving pedestrians, and looking in the shop windows at all the things she would never have dreamed of buying. Like any girl, it was the clothes shops she dawdled for most, and while looking in the window of one of the better known chain stores, she suddenly seized upon the idea of buying a new dress.

The idea took hold rapidly. In vain did she tell herself she had no use for a new dress, since she had nowhere to go to wear it; the desire to own a new dress had nothing to do with logic, and even if it had, she would simply have told herself that opportunity would present itself in time. Her window-shopping at once took on a new dimension of pleasure. She smiled to herself and went inside.

In Kestrel's past experience, when a person went to buy something to wear, one of two things happened. Either there was nothing at all in any of the shops that had the least appeal, or everything in every shop looked simply marvellous. This time the latter was the case. Kestrel wandered past rack after rack of clothes of the most appealing colours and textures, rather like a child let loose in a sweet-shop, and in the end the profusion of choice defeated her. With all that richness of pattern and colour around her, she chose in the end a plain dress of a pale cream colour.

It was a lovely dress, though. It was made of a soft, clinging material that looked and felt rather like satin, and fell in soft, classical folds, gathering slightly at the waist. Its only decoration was a little smocking in fine red threads on the bodice, which was rather demure, with its memory of childhood; but the back, which plunged almost recklessly from the neckline, was anything but demure. Kestrel bought it and took it away, and rode happily home on the train with the dress bag on her lap, filled with a pleasant anticipation, though of what she was not quite sure.

She took longer to get home than she had thought, and there was no time to go anywhere else to watch the programme—Theo and Laura had both invited her, and there was a television in both pubs—so she and her father settled down with their supper on their laps to watch the programme together. As it happened, she was glad it turned out that way, for watching herself on the television was excruciatingly embarrassing, and she could hardly look at herself. No sooner was the piece over, however, than she wished she could see it again. For all that it was herself and she had to be modest, the whole item was very impressive, and what she had thought of before as her awkwardness and stiffness came over as great authority. Her short, brisk answers to Bill Anderson's questions sounded sensible, level-headed, and quite did away with any suggestion that she was simply a sentimentalist who loved little birdies.

The harriers, too, were magnificent. The film had been just slightly edited to include all the most spectacular shots of their aerobatics, and Kestrel was surprised and pleased at how professional the film appeared—like something out of a *Horizon* programme.

'Excellent, Kestrel,' was her father's judgment when the programme ended. 'You behaved most naturally in front of the cameras, and I thought they put the ideas together very well.'

'I liked your voice over the film, telling about how you discovered them,' Kestrel said. 'It sounded just as if you were filming the birds yourself and talking while you filmed. Anyway, it must do the cause some good, and that's the main thing.'

'I wonder if anyone from the parish council was watching,' her father mused.

'I should think it quite probable,' Kestrel said. 'After all, *Roundabout* is a very popular programme.'

How popular they were to find out. About ten minutes after the end of it, the telephone rang, and Mr Richards answered it. Kestrel heard him speaking from the other room.

'Yes...thank you...most kind of you to say so...well, I hope so...no, we're having a meeting on Sunday and...yes...thank you...yes, I'll tell her.'

He rang off and came back in with a strange smile on his face.

'Who was it, Dad?' Kestrel asked.

'It was a lady who lives in Ipswich and who has just seen the programme on the television and who loves birds and who simply *had* to phone up to say she was on our side all the way and hoped we'd win, and would I tell you she thought you spoke very well.'

'No, really? How funny,' Kestrel said. 'I suppose—' and at that moment the phone rang again. 'I'll get it this time.'

This time it was a girl who had worked in the same office with Kestrel, and the call took rather longer, for she wanted to gush forth all her excitement at having someone she *knew* actually appear on the television. Kestrel listened patiently, hoping to be able to get across some propaganda, but she was defeated by the other's sheer excitement. Eventually she managed to disentangle herself and put the phone down, whereupon it immediately rang again.

For the next hour and a half the phone rang almost continuously as friends and relatives and quite a few complete strangers called up to say they had seen the programme and to congratulate Kestrel. The strangers were people who had looked up the number in the directory, or asked Directory Inquiries, and in general called to say they were very keen on preservation and very down on more building in country areas. One man did say that he couldn't understand how anyone could put a couple of birds before new houses when there were two hundred thousand homeless people in the south of England alone, but he was in a minority of one.

At last the calls petered out, and the Richards were able to relax.

'Phew,' said Kestrel, dropping into a seat. 'I didn't know so many people cared! I'm astonished that complete strangers should bother to look us up in the directory just to phone and say they agreed with us.'

'I'm glad they did,' Mr Richards said. 'It's heartening that people *do* care enough to actually do something. Those who care more for the building seem not to be bothered.'

'Nor would they,' Kestrel said vehemently. 'Nasty, soft-living, money-grubbing speculators.'

Mr Richards laughed. 'I can see the picture forming in your mind, and it's straight out of Dickens. Now, how about a cup of tea?'

'I'll make it,' Kestrel said, jumping up, and the phone rang again. Mr Richards answered it, and it was the operator, asking him if he would accept the charge for a call from a call-box in London. He listened in disbelief, and then burst out laughing.

'No, I will *not*,' he said emphatically. 'Tell them to call back tomorrow when they've got change.'

The local opinions came in the next morning. Mr Richards was working on the garden, and quite a few villagers 'dropped by' to say they had seen the programme, and what was it all about, then? One or two of them brought presents, as if it had been some kind of a celebration. Mr Richards was very touched by their attentions, and offered them tea, but the village in general was in awe of him, because of his reputation and the fact that he had written a book, and the invitations were refused shyly and the visitors went away.

Kestrel, more boldly, went out into the middle of the fray, and went down to the village where, it being Saturday morning, there were plenty of people about. She was accosted every few yards and had to explain what it was all about so often that she was glad to make the haven of Theo's shop. It proved, however, that the television had seized the local attention, even if few people had actually taken in the subject matter.

Theo revived her with coffee, and asked her about her experience.

'Well,' she said when Kestrel had finished, 'I wouldn't have known from watching you that you felt at all out of place. You seemed very much at home, very self-possessed and in control of the situation. In fact, I felt rather sorry for Bill Anderson, charming away and getting no response!'

'Oh don't,' said Kestrel, putting a hand over her face. 'You make me sound like one of those terrifying career women who won't let men hold doors open for them.'

'I'm joking, infant,' Theo said. 'Actually you looked quite neat and pretty, and quite feminine.'

'Well, never mind about me, the point is it was obviously watched by most of the village people, and a lot outside too,' and she told Theo about the phone calls.

'Jolly good! I hope you told them all to come along on Sunday to the meeting?'

'Oh yes, and told them to write to their MPs and the RSPB and the Conservation Society,' Kestrel said. 'I just hope the phone call wasn't their one burst of energy.

Anyway, we'll see on Sunday. But I think at least that the whole of the village will turn out.'

'No doubt of it,' Theo said comfortably. 'Where are you going now?'

'To do some shopping—just general food and things.'

'Well, I should be careful if I were you. I just saw three members of the WI go past in the direction of the dairy, and if you get caught by them you may have to listen to the history of Mrs Dorrit's niece's stage career.'

Kestrel groaned. 'In that case, I think I'll go along and see Laura instead.'

She headed towards the library with her head down, and was moving fast in the hopes of not being spotted when she ran smack into someone who was coming out of the library. Fortunately it was a tall person, so she only collided with his chest, which was less painful all round. Strong hands gripped her shoulders to steady her from the rebound, and she looked up into Stuart King's face, to find he was smiling.

'Hello! What's all the hurry?' he asked her.

'I was trying to avoid being waylaid

again,' she said, glancing over her shoulder. There was no-one nearby. She relaxed, and tried not to notice that he had not let go of her shoulders yet. 'I've had to explain the *Roundabout* programme about fifty times in as many yards, and I'm running out of steam.' Then she realised that he might not have watched the programme, and said, 'I don't suppose you watch television—'

'Why suppose that?' he asked her. He seemed to want to know, and waited for her answer. She couldn't say 'because you're too superior', because that would be rude, and, on reflection, probably unjust. She thought for a moment and then said,

'Because you're living in a hotel, and not at home.'

'I rather suspect that isn't your real reason—judging by how long it took you to think of it,' he said. She felt embarrassed at being caught out so blatantly, and wriggled a little, drawing attention to the fact that he was still holding her. He looked at his hands, and then at her face, which she turned obstinately away, and then tightened his grip a little.

'People staying in hotels often watch

television more than they would at home, because there isn't anything else to do, especially if they don't know anyone in the area.' She looked up at him, and found that his eyes were looking directly into hers in a way that made her feel rather dizzy. She felt herself blush, and then grow pale, and wondered quite seriously for a moment if she were going to faint, for she really felt most peculiar.

Stuart, apparently satisfied that she was not going to run away, released her from his grip and his gaze and said in a more conversational tone,

'I did see you on television—I was very impressed. You sounded so sensible and calm—quite unlike the young lady with whom I've had one or two brushes.' He paused, and then said, 'You haven't much to say for yourself this morning. I seem to be doing all the talking. It's very hard trying to start up a conversation when the other person won't respond.'

'Why should you want to start up a conversation?' Kestrel asked quickly.

'Because it occurred to me that I ought to know something about you. After all, I have been elected honorary enemy for the occasion. Here we are, ranged on opposite sides like two candidates at an election, and we've hardly even spoken to each other.'

'Is it necessary to know the enemy?' she asked.

'Is it necessary? I don't know,' he said reflectively. He had an odd way of taking rhetorical questions seriously, and answering them properly. 'I think it may add interest to the battle. Anyway, putting aside grounds of mere necessity, I would like to get to know you. You interest me.'

'You make me sound like—'

'Yes?'

'Some sort of specimen.'

'Like a bird I'm studying?' This time Kestrel caught the tremble of laughter in his voice, and realising there was a pun on the word 'bird' she glanced up, caught his eye, and started to laugh.

'That's better,' he said, laughing too. 'You're altogether too earnest for this time of the morning.'

'Life is an earnest business, Mr King,' she said solemnly, and he continued to smile at her.

'Not on Saturdays. On Saturdays we don't work—it's the weekend, time for leisure. We don't campaign either,' he added sternly, and she nodded meekly.

'What do we do then, sir?' she asked. Quite suddenly he dropped the play.

'Will you have dinner with me tonight?' he asked. She opened her mouth and shut it again, not knowing quite what to say, for she was taken aback. Of all things, she had not expected this. She began to shake her head, thinking that it was bound to end in a quarrel, but he seemed to read her thoughts and said, 'We'll make a pact before we go not to mention either birds or buildings, and that way we won't argue, except perhaps in a friendly way as people do.'

It was the word 'friendly' that did it. The idea of being his friend seemed so delightful, it bloomed and glowed in her mind like a red geranium against a grey wall.

'That,' he said very softly, 'was quite a different sort of smile. I wish I could ask you what you were thinking just then. But I won't. Will you come to dinner with me?'

'Yes,' she said. 'I should like that.'

'We'll go somewhere really nice,' he said, 'and I'll pick you up at your front door with the car, so you won't have to wear wellingtons.'

'I shan't disgrace you,' she said, hurt, and then saw he was teasing her. And, she suddenly realised, I have a new dress to wear! What did I tell you, her illogical side told her, buy the dress and the opportunity to wear it makes itself.

'I hear the Crown at Southwick does a good dinner, is that right?' Stuart asked her.

'Oh yes, it has a restaurant that's very well known round these parts. Quite as good as—' At that moment she suddenly remembered the last time she had been in the Crown, remembered something about it. 'We won't talk about birds or building?' she said.

'No, I promise. And you must promise too.'

'Oh, I promise,' she said, pushing down firmly the laughter that bubbled up inside her. 'Especially not birds.'

He looked at her with his head slightly tilted, wondering what she was planning, and then said, slightly warily, 'What time shall I pick you up? Would half past seven do?'

'Yes, that will be fine,' Kestrel said.

'I'll book the table for eight, then,' he said. He still seemed doubtful. 'You *will* be ready, won't you?'

'Yes, of course, don't worry. I said I wouldn't let you down,' Kestrel said, and by now she had succeeded in controlling her laughter, and spoke quite seriously.

'Until tonight, then,' he said, and went on his way.

Kestrel spent the rest of the day in a daze. The more she thought about it, the more extraordinary it seemed. It just didn't seem possible that she should be going out to dinner with Stuart King—that he should have asked her. And after all the pointed remarks that had been thrown at her since he arrived in the village, she went in terror of someone having seen them talking. She didn't want to have to tell anyone, and it was only with reluctance she told her father, though she knew that he would not tell anyone else.

'The Crown, eh?' was all her father said. 'You should get a good dinner, then.'

He seemed not at all surprised, and though she felt he should be, she could not bring herself, to discuss it with him. When

205

it was found out in the village—as it would be, without any doubt—that she had gone to dinner with 'the man from Norwich', there would be discussion enough, and it would be like being rubbed with a cheese-grater. She didn't want even to speak of it now.

Stuart was no less surprised than Kestrel. To get involved with her seemed like an act of madness. To go where the village had patently been pushing him seemed like an act of weakness. He could not explain it to himself, except to say that there was some strange kind of attraction about her, a wildness that pulled at him; and odder still, a familiarity about her, as if he had known her for years, as if he knew the way her mind worked and what she would say next.

'Well, at any rate,' he told himself in the mirror as he shaved that evening, 'you may find out enough about her tonight to stop you wondering.' And that, of course, would be a blessing, because she was interfering seriously with his peace of mind.

Each of them had made a special effort

with their appearance, out of a feeling of unsureness about the other, and neither of them was prepared for the effect of that special effort on their feelings.

Stuart arrived a little early, and was greeted by Mr Richards, who invited him into his study to wait, and immediately entered into a conversation with him. They discussed such pleasant matters as church architecture and jazz and types of car and which television channel had the best comedy programmes, and by the time Kestrel was heard coming down the stairs each had formed a very favourable opinion of the other.

Stuart stood up and turned towards the door as Kestrel came in, and for a long moment they looked at each other with almost painful awareness. Stuart thought he had never seen anyone so beautiful. The dress clung softly to her body, the cream setting off the dark honey colour of her skin, for she never lost her summer tan. Her hair hung round her face in soft, burnished curls; her Siamese-cat eyes glowed in her face, but her expression was gentle, almost shy. It seemed an honour that this wild, exotic creature should trust him enough to be there; he felt he must move softly, or scare her away.

And for Kestrel, it still seemed incredible that he should have asked her. He looked simply stunning, far beyond her reach, the kind of person she could only daydream about meeting—yet there he was talking to her father, the two of them getting on so well, as if they were old friends. There was a long moment of silence as they looked at each other, not knowing what would be adequate to the moment to say, and then Mr Richards spoke.

'Well, you two had better be getting along, hadn't you?'

Kestrel turned towards him, and the feelings she could not express to Stuart came out in a rush of affection for her father.

'You'll be all right on your own, won't you Dad?' Mr Richards looked rather surprised.

'Of course I will! Why not? Have a good time, both of you, and don't hurry back.'

''Bye, Dad,' Kestrel said, and gave him a bear hug and a kiss. Then she turned to Stuart. 'I'm ready.'

And they walked out to the car without looking at each other.

CHAPTER 15

The journey to Southwick was not long, but Stuart was unused to driving in the country at night, and took it slowly, letting the yellow Capri nose carefully round blind corners where Kestrel knowing what was beyond, would have zoomed. So the journey seemed longer, and since they both felt very much aware of the other's presence, they were silent, not knowing how to begin.

At last they passed the outlying cottages of the village, and Stuart said, 'It's just up here, isn't it?'

'Yes—round the next bend. Go slowly— people sometimes park on the road, though they're not supposed to.'

The silence fell again, and while Stuart manoeuvred the car into the pub's coach-yard and eased it backwards into a parking space, he felt the tension grow up between them. By the time he put on the hand brake and turned off the engine he knew he had to do something to break the tension, or the evening would be a failure, so as Kestrel put her hand out to open her door he reached over and put his hand over hers to stop her.

'What's the hurry?' he asked. His voice sounded, to him, most peculiar. She turned her face towards him. The yard was very dimly lit, but he caught the glint of her eyes as she moved her head.

'No hurry,' she said in a slightly surprised voice. 'Why?'

He reached out his hand, slid it under her hair around the back of her neck, and pulled her gently but firmly towards him. He felt her resist him at first, as if she were not sure what he was going to do—but of course she must have known. He pulled harder, and she gave way suddenly and his arms were round her. With a feeling almost of relief he kissed her—a hesitant, exploring kind of kiss. Then he held her quietly for a moment before letting her go.

She straightened up and put up a hand to her hair, but he knew it was all right.

'So that's that,' she said, but her voice in the darkness sounded pleased. 'Shall we go in to dinner?'

'By all means,' he said, and got out of

the car, and she was so relaxed that she didn't move but let him come round and open the door for her. 'You'll remember the taboo subjects,' he said as he locked the car door.

'Oh, certainly,' she said, and there was suppressed glee in her voice, and he wondered why.

They went into the bar, and efficiently he found the waitress and gave his name: 'King. Table for two at eight.'

'Oh yes, sir,' she said, consulting her list. 'Would you like to have a drink first, while I bring you the menu? Perhaps you'd like to sit over there. What would you like?'

'Kestrel?' he turned to her, feeling rather odd at using her name for the first time.

'Sherry, please. Medium.'

'Two medium sherries then, please,' he told the waitress, and he and Kestrel sat down in a comfortable corner while the waitress brought the drinks and two menus.

'This is very nice,' Stuart said, looking round the bar. 'Not too fancy, but comfortable and solid. I've heard the food's good, too.'

'It is,' Kestrel said. 'Dad brought me here for my birthday last year, and he

211

arranged with the chef to make me a birthday cake too. It was so sweet! The staff brought it to the table after the meal, with a bottle of champagne, and it was only about six inches square—the cake, I mean—and iced with my name and 'Happy Birthday'.'

'What a nice idea,' he said. 'Did your father order the champagne, too?'

'Yes, to go with the cake.'

'He sounds like a romantic,' Stuart commented.

'I suppose he is. We're very fond of each other.'

'That much is obvious. Did he choose your name?'

'Yes.' Kestrel made a face. 'It was a burden when I was small—you know how children tease you if there's anything a bit odd about you. But I've got used to it now, and I rather like it. At least it's different.'

'I think it's a lovely name, and it suits you, in some way,' Stuart said, considering her. 'Why Kestrel in particular, anyway?'

'My father's favourite bird. Hawks and falcons are his speciality. Of course, when the film came out, I got called 'Kes' all the time, and I hated it. Mostly the village people call me Kesterl.'

Stuart laughed. 'I must say, I've never had any trouble with my name. It's just dull enough for no-one to notice it.'

'It suits you, in a kind of way,' Kestrel said, and then realised how that sounded. 'I don't mean you're dull—I don't think it's a dull name. Rather dignified really.'

'And is that how you think of me—dignified?'

'Oh, terribly,' she said, smiling wickedly. 'As if one ought to pay to speak to you.'

'Dear me,' he said mildly. 'If I'd only known I could have made my fortune by now.'

The waitress came back and hovered, and Stuart smiled up at her winningly. 'I'm afraid we haven't even looked yet. Now, Kestrel, as the past expert, what do you recommend?'

'I don't—I'd hate to have that responsibility. But I know what I'm going to have—the stuffed eggs followed by the pheasant.'

Stuart glanced at her sharply, but her expression was demure. It must have been coincidence that both dishes she chose were something to do with birds.

'I'll start with the rollmops,' he said,

determined not to fall into the same trap, 'and then I'll have a steak, I think.'

Kestrel said, disappointedly. 'I don't like people to have dull things when I eat out—I like them to try out unusual dishes.'

'So you can taste a bit,' Stuart said. 'I'm on to you.' The waitress smiled patiently and said,

'And what vegetables, sir? Shall I bring a selection?'

'Yes, that would be fine.' The waitress took the menus and departed, and Stuart crossed his legs comfortably and said, 'And that gets the hard part of the evening over with, so now we can relax. I often think it would be better for restaurants to serve only one meal, so that you didn't have to make a choice. It's bound to put a strain on the evening, wondering if you've chosen right, and whether you would have enjoyed something else better.'

'Oh, I don't agree,' Kestrel said cheerfully. 'I think reading the menu is the best part.'

'Better than the eating?'

'Yes, much better. While you're reading the menu you can taste everything. Once you've chosen you're stuck with one dish only.'

'Well, then, that only goes to prove my argument. If you didn't have to choose you wouldn't be let down.'

'No, it doesn't—I said reading the menu was the best part of the evening. If they didn't give you a menu to read, you'd lose most of the pleasure. In fact, I think I'd like it best if, when you went to a restaurant, you just sat down and had menu after menu brought in, and having read them all through, you went home.'

Stuart laughed. 'That would certainly solve the world's food shortage, but it might reduce the population too drastically.'

'It would be a roaring success commercially —think of the profit margin on a meal!'

With cheerful nonsense they whiled away the time until the waitress came to tell them their table was ready, and then they got up and followed her in, and Stuart noticed again that Kestrel's body was taut with excitement. He soon found out why. At the threshold of the room he paused and regarded it with pleasure: a low, beamed ceiling, and three whitewashed walls, the fourth wall, opposite him, housing a wide brick fireplace and painted a vivid, almost peacock blue. White tablecloths on the tables, with surnaps of the same blue, and a darker blue carpet. A candelabrum on each table, with lighted candles, and a pretty sparkle thrown back from the silver and glass.

And all round the walls, framed pictures —of birds. Wrens, tits, owls, warblers, seabirds, various kinds of ducks, finches, all beautifully drawn and coloured. And on the mantelpiece of the flickering fire were two of those Victorian glass domes filled with stuffed birds in various attitudes on twigs and painted grass. No wonder Kestrel had been in internal fits of laughter ever since he had suggested the Crown as their dining place! No wonder, indeed, that her father had brought her here for her birthday dinner!

She turned now to look at him, her cheeks red with bottled-up laughter, her eyes sparkling with fun, and his heart missed a beat.

'All right,' he said huskily. 'It was my choice, I admit it!'

'I could hardly keep from laughing when you said it,' Kestrel said. 'One thing right after the other—we won't talk about birds, and let's eat at the Crown. Oh, it was lovely! And to see your face!'

'Well, now I'm here I suppose I'd better accept defeat and look at some of them. Owls, now, they strike me as pleasant enough creatures.'

'Unless you're a mouse,' Kestrel said. Stuart had strolled over to one group of pictures, and looking at them more closely he noticed, to his surprise, that they were signed in a small neat hand 'G. Richards'.

'Is the G Richards who did the drawings any relation?' he asked Kestrel as he joined her at their table.

'It's my father,' Kestrel said, looking up. 'Didn't you know?'

'I didn't know he could draw,' Stuart said. 'They're very good.'

'I thought you didn't know anything about you-know-whats.'

'Birds? Oh, I don't. I don't know if they're accurate or true-to-life. I was only thinking of them as drawings.'

'Are you interested in drawing and painting?'

'Yes, very. You sound surprised?'

'I was, a little; I didn't think of you as being the artistic type. I thought of you as being more practical.'

'I'm practical too. The two aren't

mutually exclusive, you know.'

'I suppose not,' Kestrel said, but she sounded doubtful. 'But I'm only practical, though I suppose you could say my father is both.'

'You may be practical—I haven't any evidence about that, but you are certainly not devoid of artistic talent.'

'Why do you say that?'

'Well, you are presumably responsible for the way you look tonight. You presumably chose the dress and put it on and did your own hair—unless you keep a lady's maid?'

Kestrel laughed, showing her white teeth. 'No chance. But what does that prove?'

'What I said. You look absolutely stunning—that is a kind of art form. That dress—perfect. And your hair. Anyone else might have worn jewellery with such a plain dress, and spoiled it, or gone in for something outlandish in the way of make-up, but you avoided those traps. You look—marvellous.'

Kestrel looked down at herself, a childlike response which he found rather endearing, and then looked up at him rather shyly. She had not expected such whole-hearted praise from him, but now as she looked at him and received his smile and the approving look in his eyes, it warmed her, and she felt happy and content and completely *right*.

From that moment the evening had to go well. They both forgot their previous enmity, and it was as if they had been friends for years. Kestrel found herself remembering the strange look that had passed between them on that occasion in Theo's shop, and wondered if it had been a kind of forewarning of tonight, a glimpse into the future. They talked easily, avoiding the sticky subject without effort, and Kestrel found he had an uncanny insight into her mind, and often knew what she was about to say before she said it. She found, too, that she understood him, and even when he had difficulty finding the words for something he wanted to explain she knew exactly what he meant.

It's as if we were made for each other, she thought a little wryly at one point in the evening, just as all the village decided when he first arrived. But she didn't want to think about the village, or its opinion, for that was too close to the dangerous ground. She just wanted to enjoy the evening.

The meal was very good, and they enjoyed it. Stuart even obligingly chose a dessert from the sweet trolley so that she could taste it—he had the cheesecake while she took the Black Forest gateau—and then they had coffee and she had a liqueur with it, something she had not tried before.

'Which should I have?' she asked him. 'I've never had one before.'

Stuart shrugged. 'It depends what kind of flavour you favour.' The waitress giggled at that. 'Do you like peppermint? Because if you do you could try crème de menthe.'

'I don't like the sound of that. Which one do you like?'

'That would be no guarantee that *you'd* like it,' he pointed out.

'True, but if it's the one you'd choose yourself, and it turns out that I don't like it, then you can drink it. That's what I mean by being practical,' she added.

'All right then, have cointreau,' he said, nodding to the waitress. The liqueur was brought and Kestrel sipped it cautiously, and then smiled.

'I knew I should like it,' she said. 'Our taste is so alike.'

It seemed to be from that remark that

the mood of the evening changed. Shortly afterwards the bill was brought, and it became apparent that the evening was over. They could have stopped in the bar for a drink, but after a large meal like that neither of them wanted anything to drink, and the jolly, crowded atmosphere of the bar seemed all wrong.

'Shall we go home?' Stuart asked, and Kestrel nodded without speaking. Home didn't sound a welcoming word, for it brought to mind the realisation that home for her was not home for him, that they were not old friends, that his stay in Wesslingham was only temporary.

Stuart drove back very slowly, not wanting the evening to end. The taboo subject, which they had had no difficulty in avoiding all evening, was uppermost in both their minds, and they were both wondering how their friendship was to be carried on in such adverse circumstances. Tomorrow they would be back on opposite sides, and whatever the outcome, it would break their friendship apart.

All too soon, Stuart pulled the car up outside Coats Cottage. The moon broke through the clouds as if on cue, and threw a band of silver light over the still marshes. In the distance the eastern face of the church was suddenly illumined, mysterious against the jagged clouds. They sat in silence, looking at the magical scene before them.

'Stuart,' Kestrel began at last, turning towards him, but he stopped her.

'Don't say anything,' he said urgently. 'Not yet.' And he took her into his arms again, and kissed her. But for Kestrel the magic was already spoilt, tomorrow was breaking through the flimsy barriers her practical mind had put up, and already she wanted to know *what would happen*. He felt her struggling to speak even while he kissed her, and in a moment he let her go angrily.

'Why can't you let it be?' he asked. 'You know this fight is useless. You know you can't win. Why don't you give in?'

'I won't. I can't. It's you who are wrong. How can you look out across those marshes, and still want to go on with what you're doing? Can't you see how wrong it is? You, who are supposed to love art?'

'But—'

'—and even if you weren't wrong, which you are, how can you ask me to stop caring

222

about something that's important to me? How could you want me to be that careless in my loyalties? Could you like that kind of a person?'

'You seem to have decided for me what I like and don't like,' he said, and his voice was cold, as it had been when they first met. His cold voice, that chilled her, for it was the voice of a stranger. How could I have thought we were friends? she asked herself.

'How could I have thought we were alike?' she cried out bitterly.

'We're not,' he said. 'We're quite unalike—' but Kestrel didn't wait for him to finish the sentence. She did not hear the wistfulness in his tone, she heard only the sharp, cold tones of a city-dweller, a stranger, and she bit her lip with chagrin.

'So unalike that I see no point in remaining here,' she said. 'It's late, I'd better go in. Thank you for the dinner—I did enjoy that part.'

'For you,' he said, 'the best part was over before dinner began.'

He meant only to revive a joke, remembering her remarks about reading the menu, but she misunderstood him, and got quickly out of the car, shutting the door sharply and walking into the house without another word.

If she cried afterwards in her bed, Stuart was not to know. And if he sat up for a good part of the night, staring out of his bedroom window and thinking about her, she was not to know that either.

CHAPTER 16

Kestrel slept late on Sunday morning, which was unusual for her. Mr Richards was surprised not to find her down ahead of him, and he got breakfast himself and then called her. She came down subdued, and it was not hard for him to work out what was wrong. He did not say anything, however, but offered her silent sympathy and hot coffee, for which she was duly grateful.

Thank heaven it was Sunday, she thought, and at least another day's respite from the problem of the building. There would be no work on the Sunday. As far as she and Stuart were concerned the situation was hopeless, of course. Their first evening together would be their last, for whatever happened, any friendship between them was doomed. If he stayed on in Wesslingham it would be because he had beaten her and driven away the harriers; and if she won, and the harriers were safe, he would go away from Wesslingham, because his job there would be finished.

Hard work is the best palliative for personal trouble, and Kestrel knew this well enough. After breakfast she threw open all the windows of the house and gave it a thorough sweeping from top to bottom, dusting and polishing with great energy. Mr Richards kept her silent company by cleaning the windows. After lunch they both worked in the garden, and he did not protest when Kestrel took to herself the hardest jobs, leaving him to pick and prod and examine, and generally stand around with his pipe in his mouth enjoying the cool damp air and the various distant bird cries.

Thus by teatime Kestrel was thoroughly tired, too tired to think about her troubles any more, and she had a bath to relax her aching back and then had tea with her father in his study, sitting by the fire and making toast by the blaze, to be spread with dripping and marmite.

'Feeling better?' Mr Richards asked eventually, after the third slice. Kestrel looked up at him and gave a small smile.

'Yes,' she said. 'I feel almost normal. You're a great comfort to me, Dad.'

'I'm glad,' he said. 'You've been a great comfort to me for years, ever since your mother died, so now I'm returning the favour. And now,' consulting his watch, 'I suppose I'd better get down to the village hall and help arrange the chairs and so on.'

The village hall was quite close, a new building that had been erected at their end of the village when the old hall had burned down about ten years ago. For a moment Kestrel thought of going with her father and helping until it was time to go to evensong. But then she thought of the Mrs Dorrits of the village, who'd be bound to be there, and couldn't face it. She wanted to put off the questioning as long as possible, and let her father go on his own.

Evensong was always a well-subscribed

service in Wesslingham, but even the vicar must have been surprised—and pleased—by the size of his congregation that evening. It appeared as though the whole village had turned out, with the exception of the few Romanists, and those die-hard non-churchgoers like the Pendles, who wouldn't have come if it was the Last Trump.

As Kestrel had anticipated, Mrs Dorrit and Miss O'Connor, the two she had most cause to fear, arrived late, having been at the village hall helping, and they had scarcely time to change into their cassocks and therefore no time to cross-question her, though Mrs Dorrit did ask her meaningfully if she had had a nice time last night, and she'd heard that the Crown did a good spread though it was wicked what they charged, for when all was said and done it was only food, wasn't it, and food was plentiful enough.

Then the choir formed up in pairs, sopranos in front and going down in voice order to Mr Barrow and Jim Cosser, the basses, at the back. Kestrel led with Mary Mayhew. Since the vicar was of an academic turn, the choir wore chorister's mortar-boards with their cassocks and surplices, and Kestrel always had trouble keeping hers on, with the result that she walked with her head up, like someone at a posture class. The vicar took his place behind with the two vergers, and they walked out of the vestry and into the, for once, crowded church.

Kestrel, walking at the front, always had a quick look round the church from under her eyelashes, just to see who was there, but on this occasion her eyes were drawn as if on strings straight to the last pew on the Decani side, for there was Stuart King, standing, hands folded before him, in a sober dark suit. Everything about him was properly quiet and reverent, except his eyes fixed urgently on Kestrel with an expression that had nothing to do with religion. Kestrel tried to fix her mind on the service and not to show herself up too obviously, but her eyes would not detach themselves from him, and she was glad to reach the haven of the choir stalls, where, facing inwards, she could not see him.

She tried not to wonder what he was doing there—after all, why shouldn't he go to church? In any case, since everyone else was there tonight, it would have been very dull for him, alone at the Bell. But why did he look at her so strangely, so fixedly? Was it only because she was at the head of the procession, and so the natural object to be stared at? During the service her mind wandered again and again to that back pew, though she did not look in that direction again.

After the service the choir filed out reverently, and once in the vestry scrambled quickly into their ordinary clothes again. Mrs Dorrit, who wore a great deal of clothing, and was slow in her methods, struggled in anguish with blouse buttons as she saw Kestrel dressed and ready in a flash.

'Dratted things, I s'l never get 'em done up. Don't you let vicar start without me,' she cried, terrified she was going to miss something. 'Why didn't I wear me blue, I'd've bin ready by now? Don't you let them start without me, now!'

Kestrel abandoned her without regret and, pausing only to say a word to the vicar, hurried out of the side door and down the road towards the village hall. The vicar was staying behind to usher everyone along, with the help of the vergers and one or two of the male choir members. On reaching the village hall Kestrel was gratified to see one or two cars there already, cars she didn't recognise, which meant that some outsiders had come to the meeting.

One of the cars belonged to the speaker from the RSPB, who was already inside and talking to her father. It turned out that Mr Richards knew him, having met him at various ornithological conventions, and when Kestrel heard his name—Percy Romaine—she was able to say politely that she had read one of his books, which made everything pleasant, for writers are always pleased to find they have been read.

The villagers began to straggle in, sitting in the seats nearest the back first, and only occupying the front seats when there was no alternative, in that odd way English audiences have. Kestrel, from her position by the stairs that led up to the platform, noticed quite a few strangers, smartly-dressed people in the main, who had presumably come by car from other villages or the nearby towns.

Theo and Laura arrived together, and came over to speak to Kestrel. Theo was to sit on the platform with Kestrel and was wearing a very smart chocolate brown suit in honour of the occasion. Laura nodded her greeting to Kestrel.

'Nervous?' she asked.

'A bit,' Kestrel said, 'but more for the outcome than for having to speak. At the moment I feel past worrying about having to speak.'

Laura nodded again, unsmiling. 'I hear tell you were out on the tiles last night.'

'Who on earth told you that?' Kestrel asked, and it came out rather sharper than she had meant it to. Laura's left eyebrow lifted a little.

'Stuart,' she said. There was a brief silence while Kestrel wondered how she had come to meet Stuart on a Sunday. As if Laura knew what she was wondering, she added an explanation. 'Larch met him out for a walk and brought him back for a cup of coffee.' Kestrel knew she meant this literally, and was not being whimsical, but she did not accept it. If Stuart had gone to Laura's, it was because he had intended to.

'What did he say?' she asked after a brief pause, in which she cancelled all the questions she had no right to ask. Laura's eyes behind her tinted glasses were neutral.

'Nothing of great interest. He just said

you and he were out to dinner, that's all.'

'Did he say anything about me?' Kestrel asked impulsively. She saw Laura look slightly surprised, and then Theo, who had been watching Kestrel more closely, interrupted by saying,

'Here comes the vicar. I think we'd better get up on the platform, don't you? Where are you going to sit, Laura?'

'Oh, in the front row,' she said, 'since no-one else seems to want to. I like to get a good view.'

In a few minutes Mr Truman had taken his place on the platform, and, having waited for the last-comers to seat themselves and for the murmur of conversation to die down, he stood up, taking on his natural role as chairman, and opened the meeting and introduced the people on the platform—Kestrel and her father, Theo, and Mr Romaine. As befitted a Sunday meeting, no-one in the audience called out anything, though on any other day of the week they would have joshed the vicar for introducing people whom everyone knew. As guest, Mr Romaine was called upon to speak first.

He gave a very good address which

sounded to Kestrel as though he had given it at countless meetings all over the country. The jokes were very polished, the pauses for laughter precisely calculated, the contrasting moods of seriousness nicely balanced. He spoke generally about birds, about their importance to the country, their role in the balance of nature, and how that balance had been upset in recent years by the destruction of their habitat, by the use of pesticides, by the poisoning of their food supplies, and by indiscriminate killing abroad. Altogether it was a very good and very professional speech, and it got a good reception from the audience, as it deserved.

The villagers were past judges on speakers. Going to meetings was a favourite pastime in the village, and they had been addressed on every conceivable subject from Hegelian Philosophy to Home Brewing. Whatever the subject, they would all turn up, and afterwards discuss the speakers and how well they had performed as a theatre audience might discuss the actors. If the subject matter was not too abstruse, they would discuss that too, but it was principally the entertainment value they came for.

Mr Richards knew that, and, as next speaker, he made use of it. He talked to them as one of them, as a Wesslingham man, a Suffolk man, and told them about *their* harriers, this rare breed that had *chosen* to come back (he made a point of that) to their native home from which they had been driven. In clear, simple terms he told them of the problem, and left them with the impression that something that belonged to them was being threatened by outsiders, that someone was trying to take away something of their own. It was a good address, and made its impact.

Now it was Kestrel's turn. She had listened attentively through Mr Romaine's speech, but when her father stood up she had caught sight of Stuart quietly edging in at the door and taking up a position standing at the back. There were several people standing there, mostly the hard men of the village who wanted to avoid committing themselves to the meeting, and who stood near the door so that, if it got boring, they could slip out to the Bell without making too much fuss. Stuart stood there like a hawk amongst pigeons, so noticeable, so much finer. Why had he come? He knew he was the arch-enemy. Was it enormous courage, or did he simply not care for the village and what it thought? Or did he think the village was behind him, rather than her?

She heard the vicar introduce her as next speaker, and stood up, her eyes still on that dark figure at the back of the hall, her heart full of conflicting emotions. The speech she had prepared flew out of her head, and she addressed the meeting passionately, from the heart, all her sincerity and emotion in her voice. It was a stirring, powerful speech, and when she sat down she felt drained; but it was not a good speech for the cause. Where Mr Richards had left them feeling they knew exactly what was at stake, and that it was all up to them, Kestrel left them feeling that here was something exclusively hers to worry about, a vague something that young women got excited about.

They were practical people in the main, and they weren't the kind to get excited about intangibles. Give them a practical problem to solve, like how to plough a practically octagonal field, or stack potatoes efficiently out of the wet, or protect a valuable pair of nesting birds, and they would put their minds to solving it. But address them from the heart and talk about posterity and loyalty and religion, and they felt uneasy.

The vicar now stood up to sum up and to propose the course of action and he knew, even as he spoke, that they had lost. The audience was sullen and restless, looking at each other and shrugging their shoulders, and some in the back were frankly talking about other things and not listening. When he called for a vote, a few hands went up straight away, those of the outsiders and one or two keen nature-lovers in the village. The rest of the village waited to see how the vote would go before committing itself, and that of course was fatal. A few more hands crept up reluctantly, some wavered and came down again, and one man converted his movement into a scratching of his nose, but leaving his elbow up in the air to cover himself both ways.

When it became obvious that no more hands were going to go up, the vicar counted. Kestrel stared at them in disbelief and anguish. She looked at her father, who shrugged, his face composed, and then back at the audience. Under her impassioned gaze, one or two people looked a little embarrassed, but they made no move.

The motion was defeated by eighteen votes to thirty-eight. Some people had not voted at all. 'I wonder,' said the vicar, 'if you can have realised quite how rare this bird is as a marsh breeder?'

'Well, Vicar,' said someone respectfully from the audience, ' 'tis only a little old bird after all, ent it?'

'Jobs is jobs, and houses is houses,' said someone else, and there was a general murmur of agreement.

' 'S not as if anyone was killin' it—nobody ent harmin' it at all,' said a woman from near the back. The talking broke out again, and the audience decided for itself that the meeting was over. The hards at the back made a bolt for the door, and others began to drift that way too, talking amongst themselves. Some were talking about the meeting, agreeing with the way it had gone. Others were talking about other things entirely, having already forgotten the harriers as if they had never been.

The vicar walked down slowly with Theo, talking about what they might do next, for he was a hardened campaigner, and to lose a battle was not to lose the war. Mr Richards was accompanying Mr Romaine to his car, and talking birds.

Kestrel was left where she sat, her eyes fixed on the departing audience as if she couldn't believe they would do this to her. Gradually the hall emptied.

Stuart was standing in the porch unobtrusively, watching the platform, waiting for Kestrel to move. He had intended to slip away as soon as the vote was taken, but her expression had made him pause, and now he stood uncertain, pitying her, wanting to comfort her but unable to approach her. At last she moved, came down off the platform and walked slowly through the empty hall towards the door. Stuart thought of speaking, but then realised that she would feel bitter towards him just then, and instead he drew back into the shadows of the porch.

She reached the door, and out of well-trained village habit she switched off the lights before stepping out into the porch. She passed him without seeing him, and Stuart heard her sigh. He felt great sympathy for her, for she looked so dejected, and he longed to comfort her, to put his arms round her, to solve her problems for her; but he stood still and watched without moving or speaking. She passed out into the lane, and he saw that her father had waited for her, so she was in good hands. The two dark figures exchanged a few words and walked away, and Stuart took his own departure towards the Bell.

Then, when he was about fifty yards down the lane, he thought of his Great Idea. It struck him so forcibly that he stopped in his tracks.

'Of course!' he said aloud. 'Why didn't any of us think of it?'

At once he turned right around and started to walk back, away from the village, towards the lane that led to Coats Cottage. Let them just get in and get the kettle on, and he would appear with the answer to all their problems. He let his mind dwell pleasantly on the gratitude of one member of the village in particular.

CHAPTER 17

Kestrel walked through the darkened porch of the village hall and down to the lane. Her father was waiting there for her, and as she reached him he put a hand on her shoulder, both to give and receive comfort.

'I just can't believe we've failed,' she said.

'Then don't believe it. This is only the first hurdle,' he said. She looked up at him, involuntarily shaking her head. 'My dear,' her father went on, 'don't take it so hard. There are other ways.'

They turned and began to walk homewards together.

'What other ways?' Kestrel asked. 'If the village isn't behind us, what can we do?'

'The village is not *against* us,' her father said. 'As many people didn't vote at all as voted against. They just need persuading.'

'But we haven't *time!*' she cried. 'Tomorrow's Monday—the builders will start work for sure. Look!'

And she pointed upwards at the moon riding free of the clouds into a lake of clear sky.

'We always knew the bad weather couldn't last for ever,' Mr Richards said quietly.

'And now it's over,' Kestrel said. It was not completely clear to her father exactly what she felt was over, but her voice was charged with bitterness. They walked on a little in silence, and then Kestrel's steps began to lag.

'Dad, I don't think I'll go straight home. I think I'd like to have a walk first, to clear my head a bit.'

'All right, dear. Don't be too long, will you, or I shall worry. And remember, the television programme has won us a lot of support—there is more we can do yet. It just needs thinking about.'

'Yes, I see that, Dad. I'll see you later. I won't be long.'

She broke away from him at a convenient place, climbed a wall and padded across a field to the edge of her beloved marsh. If her father was so calm about it, she reasoned with herself, why should I not be? I would be vain to think that I care more about the harriers than Dad does.

Perhaps it's just that he's older, and can take disappointments better, she thought next. She climbed the wall at the far side of the field, and stood still, looking across the moonlit scene and snuffing the night air. Last night—was it only last night?—she and Stuart had gazed at the same scene, sitting so close that they were almost touching, and yet separated by a distance greater than miles. His face was not hard to conjure, for it had haunted her all day, as vivid when he was not before her as when he was.

She loved him—she knew that now. She had to admit it to herself, seeing that her longing to be with him was making her heart ache even now, when there were other things to be cared about. But it was a hopeless love, and she should shut it out of her thoughts if she was to carry on living normally.

Or was it so hopeless? They were separated only by her love of the marsh harriers—there was nothing else to keep them apart. If she were to give up trying to protect them, forget about them, there would be no problem. After all, did it matter if they bred here or elsewhere? As the woman at the meeting had said, no-one was harming them. For a sweet, dangerous moment she allowed her mind to toy with the idea of a future with Stuart, to be brought about by her withdrawal from the campaign.

And then she shook the idea from her head angrily. How could she even contemplate it? Everything she was was bound up with the marsh and its inhabitants. From her earliest childhood she

242

had gone with her father to hide in the reed beds and watch the birds he loved. How could she abandon a cause so dear to her, so dear to her father? As she had said to Stuart herself, how could he love someone who could so lightly abandon something she had said she cared for? If Stuart were not true to his principles, she would not care for him, and she knew that the same was true for him. And, of course, it *did* matter that the harriers nested here. It was not only the harriers, though they were the focal point of the matter, but the new houses were a further encroachment on the marsh, and would be an environmental hazard to any number of species, both birds and animals.

No, it must be love that was sacrificed. He would go away in the end, one way or another, and she would forget him, in time. She was walking towards the nesting site quite automatically, stepping quietly through old habit, and keeping a sharp look-out for anything that might be out in the darkness. It was not long before she perceived that she was being followed, and looking over her shoulder she saw a low, pale shape tapering off into darkness at each extremity.

Larch stopped when she stopped, and greeted her with a loud miaou that seemed to have a slightly questioning note to it, as if he wondered what she was doing prowling around in *his* dark.

'You shouldn't make such a noise if you're hunting,' she told him. He answered with another of his Siamese noises, and on an impulse she stooped and picked him up. Larch didn't like to be held, and normally would have evaded her neatly, but for once he allowed the liberty and lay across her shoulders staring away from her indifferently as she stroked him. But his purr, like a small engine, gave him away.

They were quite close to Laura's bungalow, and Kestrel could see a pinprick of light through a gap in the thorn hedges which she guessed was from the window of Laura's back kitchen.

'Was that where you were going?' she asked Larch. 'Back home to missus?' If she went there, Laura would say that Larch had found her and brought her home. Kestrel's mind went back relentlessly, and she found herself wondering again why he had been there. Just friendliness? Where else did he have to go, after all? Or was it more than that?

244

With a shove of his powerful back legs Larch freed himself and jumped down, trotting out ahead of her on what was, to him, a well-worn path, his tail straight up in the air like a standard. Kestrel followed him without noticing.

Would he be there now, with Laura, laughing at her dry jokes, taking supper with her perhaps, helping with the washing-up afterwards, conversing while he dried the dishes? Larch had brought her to the back fence, and here she paused, staring at the house with unseeing eyes.

What business was it of hers, anyway, she suddenly asked herself. Larch said 'prrp?' inquiringly over his shoulder, and she said aloud,

'Not this time, cat,' and turned in her tracks. She had walked enough, thought enough, and now it was time to go home. It was none of her damned business how Stuart, or Laura, spent their spare time, and she must just fix her mind on the next thing to be done and forget about him.

A brisk walk brought her home to the back yard of Coat's Cottage, and she smiled to herself as she saw the vicar's motorbike propped up against the wall. He must have gone home first, she reasoned, because he hadn't had the bike with him at the meeting. He must have gone home after the meeting, and then been struck with a new idea for the campaign and come zooming down to discuss it.

Or perhaps he had merely wanted to talk, perhaps to stimulate ideas. The light streaming out from the study window told Kestrel that they were sitting in there as usual, and also that her father had forgotten to draw the curtains. Now she was home she felt strangely reluctant to go in, as if that would be an irrevocable decision, as if it would bring about some action that she would sooner put off. She hesitated in the dark for a moment, and then walked quietly round to the window to look in, unobserved.

Her father was walking about the room, talking as he walked. He liked to move about when he was thinking something out, and she had often teased him and told him he looked like an American executive dictating to his secretary. The vicar was sitting in an armchair by the fire, almost facing the window, looking up at her father and adding comments or asking questions from time to time.

On the other side of the fire, with his

back to her, sitting in the other armchair, was someone else, someone tall and young; the back of a beautiful neck; dark hair with a slight wave to it. The back of that head she would recognise anywhere. But what was he doing there? Her first impulse was to rush in, just to be near him, but she stayed it. Had he come to gloat? No, unworthy of him. Anyway, the conversation seemed to be friendly, if serious. What on earth could they be saying? If only she hadn't gone for a walk she could have been here when he arrived, she could have spent those ten or fifteen minutes in his company.

So much for him being with Laura! Laura's cat had been like a decoy to lure her away from him. The fates were against her! But in any case, she remembered suddenly, she had already decided to drive him out of her thoughts. So what was she getting excited about? She could not take pleasure in his company any more.

She felt suddenly tired, and wanted only to be in her own room, safe and alone, away from anything anyone could say to her. She left the window and went round to the side door, entering silently and closing the door behind her gently so that she could go up to her room unnoticed. She had just put her foot on the stairs when she realised that she would have to tell her father she was back, or he would wait up for her. She paused, and then resignedly turned back to the study and went in at the open door.

She had made no sound, but at once his eyes were drawn to her as if by some kind of magnetism. He stood up, his eyes never leaving her, and the vicar and her father looked round to see what he was staring at.

'Ah, Kestrel, you're back,' said her father. 'Good. Mr Truman came round to discuss what our next plan of action should be, and then we were honoured with another visitor.' He nodded towards Stuart. Kestrel did not look at him. She kept her eyes on her father and said,

'Yes, Dad. I just came in to tell you I was back. I think I'll go straight up to bed—I'm rather tired.'

'Oh, not yet, my dear. Come in and sit down for a while,' said her father. The vicar had also stood up and was offering her his chair, and Kestrel looked at him vaguely, aware almost exclusively of the tall dark figure on the edge of her vision.

'Mr King came to us with an idea. You must hear what he has to say.'

'I don't think I could be interested in anything Mr King has to say,' Kestrel said. 'I really am very tired. Goodnight.'

And she turned away before anyone could say anything else, and ran upstairs to her bedroom.

In the study the three men stared after her, and then looked at each other inquiringly.

'I'm afraid she took our defeat rather hard,' the vicar said.

'I'm sorry about that,' Mr Richards said to Stuart. 'She's probably still a bit upset. I thought she would walk it off but—'

'It's all right,' Stuart said. 'I understand.'

'She'll be calmer tomorrow. There'll be plenty of opportunity to tell her then,' said Mr Richards. 'It's a pity to let her spend another night in that state, I suppose. Perhaps I'd better go up to her later.'

'If you'll excuse my saying so,' Mr Truman said, 'if Kestrel is feeling rather overwrought, it may be better not to raise her hopes before we are sure of success. Tomorrow would be better.'

'You're right. I'll tell her tomorrow,' Mr Richards said.

As it happened, he didn't get the chance. Kestrel spent a restless night, and woke up even earlier than was her usual habit. Her head ached and she felt miserable, and she decided at once to get up and go out for a walk. The sky was already clear blue, the sun was just coming up, and it was obviously going to be a beautiful day. She would go out and enjoy it, for this was the last chance to enjoy such weather. After eight o'clock, the weather would be a curse, and her day would be spoilt.

She dressed in her jeans and a tee-shirt of a faded and delicate shade of blue and crept quietly out of the house without waking her father. She walked deliberately away from the site of all her troubles, and headed in the general direction of Southwick and the river for a long walk. The marsh was teeming with life, for this was the active time of the year, and the promise of a fine day had brought out other creatures besides herself.

This was the best time of day, before anyone else was about. At this time of day she felt she belonged with the world of nature, that she was a part of it, and not an unnatural intruder from the world of

250

men. The flat green land by the side of the river was dotted with seagulls, all sitting facing the wind as was their wont, which gave them a curiously orderly appearance. Some of them moved a step or two as she passed, but on the whole they accepted her and stayed where they were.

It was still too early for people to be about, and she saw only one other human—in the distance, a fair girl riding a white horse over towards the railway line. The first train of the day came by, and Kestrel watched, amused, as the girl spurred her horse into a gallop and raced the train until her way was blocked by the fringe of trees and she was forced to pull up. Kestrel saw her raise a jaunty arm in salute to the train as it pulled away from her.

Her walk took her in a long, irregular half circle as the day broadened. She had no watch on, but she knew by the feel of the morning that it was well past seven, going on eight. She walked more slowly, as if to stretch out the time, and, without her even realising it, her walk was taking her back to the village and the building site. As she came within sight of the church, it struck eight. Unwillingly, she walked on, drawn towards the place where she must witness the end of their hopes of the harriers.

She kept well out, making a wide loop round the nest site out of cautious habit. She could hear no machines yet—perhaps they were late starting. The church clock now stood at half past eight. She was in sight of the place now, and there was no-one there. No-one at all—no workmen, no machines, just the piles of bricks and the little hut and the wood and string markers where the foundations would be dug.

Kestrel paused, puzzled. The day was so fine she had thought they would make an early start. She crept closer, working her way round under cover like an animal, keeping close by the hedges. Ah, there was someone, at last, just coming into the yard from the street. Kestrel's heart gave an uncontrolled leap as she saw that it was Stuart. She thought she understood now—he had come to inspect the ground and see if it was dry enough, and then he would phone the builders and tell them to come in and start.

She watched him as he walked across the yard, looking round him, pausing to pick up a piece of rubbish, stepping over a puddle. He seemed relaxed and at ease, in no hurry at all. He wasn't even making any show of examining the place. He looked more like a person who had come out for a walk and had crossed the building site by sheer chance. In fact, he was coming towards her now, as if he intended walking on the marshes. Kestrel had been still, watching him and drinking in the sight of him as if it could quench a thirst in her, but now the danger of being discovered made her move.

She backed carefully towards the cover of the hedge, but though she thought she had been silent, she must have made some slight noise, for his head turned at once towards her and he began to walk in her direction. She moved backwards still, but a moment later he came round the bushes and was standing there only feet away.

'Kestrel,' he said. Her heart was bounding about uncomfortably at his presence, and at the sound of her name on his lips. But she wouldn't show him she was discomposed. She drew herself upright and stared at him. 'Why are you hiding?' he asked. 'Why do you keep running away from me?'

'I'm not,' she said. It didn't sound convincing even to her.

'But why do you look so miserable? I'm not still the enemy, am I?'

'You should know best about that,' she said. He looked quizzical.

'Hasn't your father told you? No, I see that he hasn't. Listen to me, I have something to tell you.'

'I don't want to hear,' she said.

'Yes, you do,' he said firmly. He reached out and took her unwilling hand, and drew her with him towards a heap of timber. 'Sit down,' he said kindly, and when she did not he pushed her down, gently, as if she were a child. 'I have the answer to the problem,' he said. 'Yes, don't look so startled, you know what I mean. It came to me last night when I was on my way back from the meeting.'

'I didn't think there could be an answer to the problem without one or other of us giving in,' Kestrel said. She wanted to warn him that she wouldn't.

'Ah, that was the whole point,' he said. 'There wasn't an answer to the problem, because we had got the wrong problem. You see, its obvious that the people who have bought this land to build on are not going to be put off for the sake of a bird. No, don't jump in with both feet—let me finish. They're going to build here, and nothing will stop them, unless the land is proved unsuitable, which it isn't.'

'So?' she said. 'Where does that leave us?'

'It then occurred to me that all along you had been demanding that the building project be cancelled completely, permanently. But the birds wouldn't be here permanently. It occurred to me that all you really wanted was for the building to be stopped while the birds were nesting and rearing their young. In fact, what you wanted was not cancellation, but postponement.'

He paused, and Kestrel's face slowly overspread with a radiant smile as she realised what he was saying.

'Of course! What fools we've all been!' she cried.

'Smile like that again for me some time, will you?' Stuart said softly.

'What?'

'Never mind. So I went to see your father, and he agreed with me that that would serve the purpose quite as well—all that was needed was to put off the building until the harriers' young had hatched and learned to fly.'

'And can that be done?' Kestrel asked.

'I think I can do it. If I go up to Norwich to see my boss I think I can persuade him that the ground is still too wet, and that it would be better to wait until the dry season before starting.'

'When will you go?'

'Today—no sense in delaying. I've already suspended the building operation, so if I'm successful in my mission your birds will be safe.'

'Oh, that's wonderful!' Kestrel exclaimed, jumping up. 'Then what are you waiting for? What are you doing here?'

'I came mainly to make sure the builders had called off, but I also thought I might see you,' Stuart said. 'I'm glad I did.'

'Well, don't hang around any longer—please, I mean. Please go straight away. I can't bear the suspense.'

'All right. I'll drive in—that'll be quicker.'

'When will you be back? When will I know?' Kestrel asked him urgently, walking with him to the road.

'I should be back this afternoon. You'll be the first to know,' he told her. Then he hesitated, looking down into her vivid face. 'Why didn't you let your father tell

256

you last night?' he asked.

'I couldn't bear to talk to you,' she said. 'Everything seemed so hopeless.'

'Everything? Do you mean—'

'Oh please go,' Kestrel begged him. 'There'll be time for all the explanations later.'

'Yes, of course there will,' he said softly. He took one last long look at her to sustain him on his journey, and then left, and Kestrel, alight with hope again, watched him until he was out of sight round the bend in the road.

CHAPTER 18

The day seemed endless. There seemed to be nothing to do, and Kestrel spent her time wandering round the village talking to people. She no longer wanted to avoid them—the new hope made her talkative, made her love everyone. She wandered from place to place, discussing the meeting and the future of the campaign with each villager she met, not mentioning the new turn of events but listening patiently as each one who had not voted for her attempted to excuse himself and justify his letting her down.

Mr Baldergammon, who had in fact voted on both sides just to be sure, was ready to speak for or against the motion depending on who came into the post office first, or on whether or not his wife was listening. When Kestrel came in, therefore, for a quarter of sherbert lemons—a present for Mr Ambrose when she passed by Dodman's again—he was strong on sympathy and condemning the waverers who didn't vote at all. Ten minutes later he was agreeing with Mr Barrow that it was a good job the vote went the way it did.

Theo was encouraging, talking of widening the campaign, and proposed a drink in the Bell, as it was going on lunchtime. Mr Partridge, who had attended the meeting since Mrs P had volunteered to look after the bar, said that the chap from the RSPB had been a good speaker and offered them both a drink on the house, which was his way of saying he was sorry.

'Meeting was good for trade, anyway,' he said. 'We had nigh on everyone in here afterwards arguing it all out again.

Nothing promotes the thirst like a good old ding-dong. Talk about custom—poor old Joe Lambert couldn't have had more'n a handful down the Dog and Duck.'

When Theo decided she had to go, Kestrel walked on through the village and stopped at the library to see Laura, and found her dealing patiently with Mrs Dorrit who was complaining that a book she had just had out was 'nothing but filth, right to the last page'.

'You did ask for something passionate,' Laura pointed out gently.

'I should ha' known from the cover,' Mrs Dorrit grumbled. 'Girls with bare shoulders like that, and under palm trees as well.'

Laura suggested that she might have bare shoulders because it was hot, palm trees generally growing in hot climates.

'I could tell from the first page it was filthy,' Mrs Dorrit said indignantly, and Laura smiled.

'Then surely you were only giving yourself unnecessary distress to read it all through?'

'Well, I—'Mrs Dorrit began, but she couldn't think of anything to say to that. 'There should be a warning on the cover, that's all I say,' she said, and stalked magnificently out.

'Government warning — reading can damage your health.' Kestrel said when she had gone, and giggled.

'She'd be furious if she asked for passion and didn't get it,' Laura said. 'But I think it was probably a little too hot for her. Especially in this weather, and in those tight corsets.'

'Hush, you make me laugh,' Kestrel said. 'It isn't kind.'

'And what makes you full of the milk of human kindness this morning?' Laura said.

'It's a lovely day.'

'You have been known not to care.'

'And the builders aren't building today.'

'Ah. That accounts for it.'

'You didn't vote yesterday,' Kestrel said. 'I'm curious—why?'

'I told you why before—I don't think you've a hope. I didn't vote against it either.' Laura's eyes were neutral, as ever. 'Mr Baldergammon voted twice, did you see?'

'The old hypocrite,' Kestrel laughed. She could forgive anyone anything today.

'When are you coming round for a game

of cards, anyway? You haven't been round for over a week. And as I remember you won last time. It's considered polite to give your victims a chance to win back what they've lost.'

'What about tomorrow night, then?' Kestrel said.

'Okay—why not tonight?'

'I just might be busy tonight,' Kestrel said, trying not to look too happy.

'Just as you like—tomorrow night it is. Come to tea.'

'Fine. See you then.'

Outside again, she walked on through the village, and arrived at length at the building site, and here she sat down on the same pile of timber as she had that morning, and fell into a day-dream. And here it was that Stuart eventually found her on his return from Norwich.

'Hullo! I thought you'd be at home waiting for me,' he said, coming over to stand in front of her. She smiled up at him, somnolent in the afternoon sun.

'How did you find me?' she asked lazily.

'Telepathy,' he said. 'Aren't you going to ask me how I got on?'

'I don't need to,' she said happily. 'I

261

can tell from your face that it isn't bad news. How did you do it?'

'I just told him quite straightforwardly the state of the site and the ground and the uncertain weather conditions and so on. The voice of reason, you know.'

'And what did he say?'

'He said that I was probably right, and how about leaving things be for a couple of months until the dry season.' Stuart sat down beside her and stretched out his legs. 'I didn't think he'd agree, as easily as that, especially since it's so fine today, but I think he's lost interest in that site rather, since it started to go wrong.'

'So there'll be no work on the site until—?'

'Two months at least,' Stuart said. 'Is that enough? Are you happy?'

'It seems to be the answer to everything,' Kestrel said, smiling at him. 'The birds will be safe. Oh, I'm so happy! Let's go and tell Dad now. You're absolutely wonderful, a genius. I could kiss you!'

Stuart caught her hand as she jumped up, and said,

'You could, you know.'

With astonishment he saw all the happiness fade out of her eyes.

'What is it? What's the matter?' he asked anxiously. She shook her head. 'Tell me,' he insisted.

'If the building is to be postponed—you'll be going away,' she said. He looked at her with growing realisation.

'Would you mind?' he asked her gently. She drew back her hand and he let it go, and sat looking at her, at her lovely wild face and bright eyes, and the proud uprightness of her stance. 'Norwich isn't all that far away,' he said. 'We could still meet sometimes, you know.'

'Yes, perhaps we could,' she said coolly. *She* was not going to beg. 'Anyway, let's not bother about that now. Let's go and tell my father the—good news.'

He fell in beside her and they walked back to the road where he had left his car.

'Kestrel,' he said, 'it occurs to me—'

'Yes?'

'I've never even seen these birds, except on the television. Would it be possible for me to see them? Would you take me sometime when they're there?'

Kestrel forgot her pride, and was only too glad to have another chance to be with him, before he went away for good.

'Yes, of course. Why not tonight? It's best to go around sunset, and it looks as though it will be a fine night. How strange—' she broke off.

'What?'

'I've just realised, I don't have to be sorry any more about the weather being good. It seems to be an age since I was last able to say what a lovely day it was.'

'I think I shall always remember you best in the rain,' Stuart said. 'Every time I saw you, you seemed to be walking about bareheaded in a downpour.'

'Looking scruffy and dirty and thoroughly unsophisticated,' Kestrel said with a hint of sharpness.

'Well, if that's the way you see yourself—'

'How else would you put it?'

'Oh no, you mustn't fish for compliments,' Stuart said. Kestrel bit her lip. She must not quarrel with him—this might be their last time together, and, for all her resolutions, she wanted to make the most of it.

'Come home to tea,' she said quickly, 'and then we'll go and see the harriers together.'

'Thank you,' he said politely. 'I'd like that.'

Mr Richards was, of course, delighted with the way things had turned out, though his immediate next question was also whether Stuart would be going away.

'I'll have to go back to Norwich,' Stuart said, 'and then I'll be sent wherever I'm needed. It's never very far away, though—I'm not one of these chaps who's back and forth to the Sahara or anything like that. All my jobs are in and around Norwich.'

'So we shan't lose you entirely?' Mr Richards asked.

'Not if you don't want to.'

'Speaking for myself, I would be very happy if you would come and visit whenever you can—and I'm sure Kestrel agrees with me.'

They both looked at Kestrel, who said desperately, 'More tea, anyone?' She didn't want him to visit occasionally—she wanted him to be with her all the time; but if he didn't feel that way about her, then what was the point of it?

Mr Richards was a tactful soul, and when Kestrel suggested it was time they went out to see the harriers, he offered his binoculars and declined to accompany them. 'I've some things I must do—some notes to write while the mood is upon me,' he said. 'You two go. We shall all have plenty of opportunities of seeing them. I might go out later.'

Kestrel and Stuart set off in silence, going the shorter way over the marshes.

'It's going to be a red sunset,' Stuart said after a while, to make conversation. 'That's supposed to be a good sign, isn't it?'

'Yes,' said Kestrel automatically. 'Red sky at night, shepherd's delight, that's the saying. It usually works, too.'

'So many of these old country sayings are based on sound science,' he said. 'I remember as a child slapping spiders' webs on a cut to stop it bleeding, and a spider's web is practically pure penicillin—so it does work.'

Kestrel looked at him in surprise. 'Fancy you knowing something like that,' she said.

'Oh, I'm not such an ignoramus as you think,' he said.

'And yet you said you knew nothing about birds.'

'I don't really. Insects were what I was always interested in. I had a marvellous collection of spiders when I was about ten.'

Kestrel laughed, scaring a blackbird out of a hedge nearby. He rattled off an alarm call as he flew low out from the bush. 'You never cease to astonish me,' she said.

'I hope I never shall,' he said, and she stopped laughing, a little shy, not knowing quite how to take that.

As they approached the site, Kestrel saw one of the harriers straight away. 'We'd better circle wide,' she said. 'There's not much wind tonight, and every sound will travel. We don't want to scare them.'

They moved in a cautious sweep and arrived at Mr Richards' hide without disturbing anything. Kestrel took the glasses first, and after a moment handed them to Stuart.

'The female's in the nest, look.'

Stuart looked. 'Which is which?' he asked, speaking in a whisper, taking his cue from her.

'The female has the paler head,' Kestrel said. She took the glasses back from him. 'I wonder if she's laying already?'

And then, as they watched, the birds once again did their aerial display, the wonderful flying circus that they had done for the television cameras. Stuart watched, spellbound, not even troubling to take the binoculars when Kestrel offered them to him.

The display ended, the female flew back to the nest, and the male perched on a fence post by the deserted building site. Stuart took the glasses again and looked through them, adjusting the focus to bring the bird sharply up before his eyes. He looked so close that Stuart almost felt he could have ruffled the feathers with his hand—had he dared. He stared at the proud head, the fierce curved beak, the bright golden eyes, ever watchful, that could pick out the tiniest movement of a fieldmouse from the height and speed of his flight. The beautiful, rich brown plumage, the strong curved feet—there was something so complete, so wild and free and untrammelled about the harrier, that he could understand why it was precious.

He put down the glasses reluctantly and turned to Kestrel.

'I could watch it for ever,' he said. Kestrel's face turned up to him, gladly. 'I understand now why it was so dear to you, why you cared so much.'

The sun had gone down now, and the long marsh twilight had begun.

'I'm glad,' she said. 'I always felt it was

wrong that you didn't see it. A person like you ought to care about beautiful things. Especially birds—especially my harriers.'

'I do care about beautiful things,' he said. 'There's one beautiful creature that's dearer to me than all the others.'

'A bird?' Kestrel asked softly, but she knew the answer. Her eyes were luminous in the dusk.

'Of sorts. The bird of my heart.' He smiled. 'I don't know where I am with you. I hardly know if I dare touch you.'

For answer she took a step closer, and then she was in his arms. 'I don't want you to go away,' she said desperately. 'I didn't mean to say it, but I can't help it.'

'Why didn't you mean to say it?' he asked, kissing her brow tenderly.

'Because you didn't seem to mind.'

'Of course I minded. I don't want to leave you, but you seemed so hostile. I suppose it's just your way. You're a wild creature, aren't you?'

'Wild and free like the harriers? No, I don't think so—not any more.' Her next words were muffled by his chest. 'I just want to be with you. It's been all I've wanted since—that time we met in Theo's shop.'

He hugged her tighter, and she gloried in it. To be held by him seemed to her all she could ever want.

'But what shall we do?' she asked after a moment, practicality seeping upwards in her mind, as always. 'You'll have to go away.'

'There's only one thing we can do,' he said, and he released her enough for him to be able to look at her. 'We'll have to get married.'

Her lips trembled. 'And then what?' her voice was no more than a whisper.

'We'll find somewhere to live—somewhere near here, near the march. I can travel in to Norwich from here—it isn't too bad a journey.'

'Won't you mind not living in the town?'

'Of course I won't, you little fool,' he said, and she was not insulted.

'Dad will be pleased if we don't move too far away,' she said. 'He likes you.'

'And you? Do you like me?'

'No,' she smiled. 'I love you.'

She lifted her face to him, and his cool lips came down on hers, and time stood still for them. Neither of them saw the harriers fly away, nor the last red fade out of the western sky; they did not feel the first touch of the dew-fall, nor observe a cautious coypu make his way towards the reed beds beyond them.

And when at last they were able to detach themselves from each other enough to begin the walk home, the whole sky was filled with stars. Kestrel looked up from the sheltering curve of Stuart's arm with wonder.

'It's going to be another glorious day tomorrow,' she said.

This Large Print Book for the Partially sighted, who cannot read normal print, is published under the auspices of

THE ULVERSCROFT FOUNDATION